SING

SING

And Other Short Stories

Dan Szczesny

The Hobblebush Granite State Short Story Series

Volume I

HOBBLEBUSH BOOKS

Brookline, New Hampshire

Composed in Dante MT and Gil Sans at Hobblebush Books

Printed in the United States of America

Cover photo by Meenakshi Gyawali of art found in Art Alley in Rapid City, South Dakota

ISBN: 978-1-939449-08-5
Library of Congress Control Number: 2015932909

"Blue Lady" was previously published in *The Buffalo Spree*.

The Hobblebush Granite State Short Story Series, Volume I
Editors: Sidney Hall Jr. and Kirsty Walker

HOBBLEBUSH BOOKS
17-A Old Milford Road
Brookline, New Hampshire 03033
www.hobblebush.com

Contents

ACKNOWLEDGMENTS *vi*

Little Warriors *1*

Gold Dust *16*

By Hammer and Hand *30*

Afternoon Television *34*

Reptile Dreams *48*

More Than Breath *66*

Blue Lady *79*

Imagine the Universe Beautiful *83*

Sing *93*

The Last Jehu *123*

Acknowledgments

This book may be filled with fiction, but all stories have origins. So I begin by paying thanks to all the fishermen, cab divers, tour operators, hikers, pilots, farmers, park rangers, cowboys, writers, cooks, carnies and kids who I had the honor and privilege of meeting along the road of life. I hope you can see a little bit of yourselves in the tales that follow.

To the mighty creatives at Spaghetti and Writers, The Berlin Writers' Group and The Blank Page. Many of these stories were torn to shreds and put back together, better, because of the fine talents at all these writing groups.

To Sid Hall and Kirsty Walker at Hobblebush. I am honored to be selected as the first writer in what will be an amazing, and much needed, series of very fine books.

To my editor, Lisa Parsons, who is cranky and combative and has no patience for shortcuts. She forces the best out of me.

To my family. Now, more then ever, you have surrounded me with support, guidance and enthusiasm. Thanks Dad, Andrea, John, Ben, Max, Kiran, Rita and Sandeep. Thanks Mom.

To my fans, my first readers, my fellow writers, the many librarians and anyone who has taken the time to come to a talk, or signing, or slide-show, thank you for giving me a chance to live this incredible life.

To the talented Tim Horvath, Mike Morin and Becky Dennison Sakellariou for having the patience to provide their kind words about the book.

To my dear friend and mountain partner, Neil Lovett. We have been to Hell and back, and still keep returning.

To Janelle, my muse, you never stop impressing and inspiring me. To Aaron, your pure heart gives me hope and fills me with wonder.

To my baby, Uma, seven pounds of light and energy.

And finally to Meenakshi, for your limitless bravery and depth of strength, I am beyond grateful.

To the girl with the fish-shaped eyes, Meenakshi

"For people who must live from day to day, past and future
have small relevance, and their grasp of it is fleeting; they live
in the moment, a very precious gift that we have lost."

—PETER MATTHIESSEN

"It never failed to amaze me how the most ordinary day could
be catapulted into the extraordinary in the blink of an eye."

—JODI PICOULT

Little Warriors

THE SLAT DOES NOT RETRACT.

Lucy Lee pulls the knob again and waits for the comforting bang that signifies her Helio's speed is dropping, but nothing.

"Come on girl, not now."

A sharp crosswind jams the plane hard, causing the engine to sputter. Not much of a blip, but to Lucy that sound might as well be a death knell. She'd expected the storm. Her plane is designed for weather just like this: low-vis, icy sleet. Just slow the plane down, make her easier to handle. Get closer to the tundra and fly in under the wind.

She curls her fore and middle fingers under the knob, counts to three, and yanks again. Nothing.

In frustration she pulls hard on the knob again and again, nearly tearing it out of the control panel.

"Hell's kitchen!"

A chunk of hail the size of a golf ball hits the plane's windshield and sprays ice over the fuselage, causing her to jump. Lucy grabs the radio and pushes the call button.

"Koyukuk, this is Helio O-3-niner. I have a non-operative slat, repeat a—"

Turbulence hits the plane so hard, the mic is knocked out of her hand. Her restraints keep her from floating out of her seat as the plane loses altitude. The red ground-speed light clicks on.

"I'd slow you down if I could," Lucy says to the flashing button. "But that ain't happening right now."

She stretches her neck to look out the side window, trying to get her bearings, but the rain and ice exploding against her plane like popcorn kernels are making it impossible to see anything. She got caught too high. Now dead reckoning is impossible unless she can find the Yukon River. And without functional slats to slow the plane, she's literally out of control in a cloud.

"Come on now, girl, how hard can this be?"

Lucy's been flying for Alaska Air for six years; this plane, her plane, the *Little Warrior*, since the start. She hears a thump behind her. One of the latches keeping her single piece of cargo from sliding has snapped. It bangs against the back of her seat so hard it jars her head forward.

It is a single coffin, a pine box.

She freezes for a moment. Try to fix the box or get the plane out of the cloud? Her choice is made for her when a blast of rain shatters the window to her right, and a cold shear of wind nearly pulls the controls out of her hands. Ice stings Lucy's forehead and cheek like pin pricks. The Little Warrior can no longer fight the storm. The plane tips hard left, bursts out of a cloud bank into open air, and Lucy gasps when she sees the black muck of the tundra only a hundred feet below her plane.

"I'm sorry, my friend," Lucy says, addressing her lifeless cargo, "but you ain't going to make your funeral. I might make mine, though."

She tightens her harness, searches frantically for flat open ground and gets ready to meet the dirt.

Two weeks before the *Little Warrior* crashes into the mud, Jimmi Oleata swings his ax high into the cool morning air, the axhead pausing for a long second, the yellow glint of the sun blinding him for a moment. Then, momentum brings the tool down, solidly, splitting the stump head cleanly, the ax burying itself deeply into the ground. The force of the impact sends a pleasant vibration up Jimmi's arm and into his shoulders.

That feeling, that tiny sense of accomplishment, is all he has now. He lifts the two halves, one under each arm, and trudges back up the berm to the waiting flatbed.

"Ataboy, Jimmi!" His uncle, drunk as always, sits against a filthy tire, smiling like an idiot. Uncle Jess is a small man, his face craggy and deeply lined. His nose is veined and cracked from the effects of Chorzi, a tribal grain alcohol made from corn pulp and roots.

Jimmi ignores him.

"You got muscles, Jimmi, look at you, and only sixteen." Jess speaks to his nephew in the broken dialect of Lower Ahtna, a dead and worthless language as far as Jimmi is concerned. "And you're not even a man yet!"

Jimmi feels his cheeks burn red. "Speak English, old man! No one cares about your tribe anymore."

Jess just howls with laughter. "Your tribe, too, Jimmi, your tribe too!"

Stumps are all Jimmi has for work now, here in the lower delta of the Kaiyah Mountains. The loggers are long gone, leaving behind plains of stumps. Since he was thirteen, Jimmi has been working these plains, loading dead tree stumps and roots into his uncle's barely functional truck and hauling them far and wide over the delta to villages that need firewood for the coming winter. There's not much left now. Jimmi has to go farther and farther from his home in Koyukuk to find the wood. Farther and farther each year, until the toil and the effort no longer are worth the few bucks village elders are able to scrape together to pay.

And his uncle, the only family he's ever really known, is useless.

"I remember a time when our people were proud, and we didn't have to dig up roots to get by," Jess is rambling, gesturing wildly to the air. "Now . . ." He flings his hands out to the wide, empty field and his voice trails off.

Jimmi just grunts, and turns back to his ax.

Lucy is floating high above her childhood home in Manila. Her mother, an American missionary, is singing. Or maybe she's muttering some mantra, a prayer? "Mama, what?"

Then free-fall, like strings being cut, she's falling into the ghetto of her neighborhood, the red tin roofs of her shanty town coming up to meet her. She can smell the floating garbage below the slats of the tin houses, the stagnant Pasig River, hear the sound of chickens.

She spreads her arms and opens herself to the water. As she hits the river, the garbage and oil and bones sting her face and arms and turn cold, like freezing rain. Suddenly her leg is on fire with a searing pain that drives her to consciousness and she yells out, grips her leg, and realizes that she's upside down. The *Little Warrior* is upside down. Through the pain, and what she realizes is blood in her eyes, Lucy scrambles to unlatch her harness and falls onto the inside roof of the plane, now covered in thick, sticky mud. As she falls, her left leg bangs against the cracked steering column and it feels like the skin below her knee has been dipped in acid. She gasps, unable to catch her breath.

Around her, the ice and rain whip through her shattered plane, her poor beautiful girl now a twisted wreck. And through her tears and the sting of ice, she sees a jarring image. The coffin has opened, and the occupant's pink, thick hand seems to reach out toward her, palm up.

Lucy screams and screams, praying for unconsciousness that never comes.

Jimmi leans hard into his adze, smoothing the side of his dugout canoe, getting it ready for the winter. This year's will be his first hunt, finally the season he's able to leave the village like a man.

4

Traditionally, the few dozen men of the village will leave, up river, for weeks to trap and hunt and bring back game. For his first time, he'll have to stay with Jess, in Jess's cabin. But he plans to set out on his own from there, to begin the project of building his own hunting lodge, farther upstream.

Two months ago, he left the village for nearly a week to stake his own claim of hunting ground, to find a good spot near the Yukon River. Now, once his own canoe is ready, he'll begin the slow task of floating the needed materials up. The cabin itself might take three or four seasons to build.

The spruce that now forms the body of his dugout came from someplace upriver, a blowdown perhaps or a low-to-the-ground lightning strike. He found the huge log near where he wants to build his cabin, and spent two days floating it back down to the village.

The tools are his father's. His father, who died face down in a mud flat, stinking of alcohol like Jimmi's uncle. His father, who beat his mother so severely that she ended up in a rez clinic with brain damage that left her out of her mind for two years before she died. His father, who never taught Jimmi how to build or forage or use a hammer. Jimmi did that himself, slowly grinding his hands into thick, meaty pulps, slowly turning his body hard as the tree stumps he chops for a living.

Now, his time has come. Now, he'll prove to them all that he can be a better man than either his father or his uncle. Now is the time of the hunt.

Through increasingly blurring vision, Lucy sees her ankle twisted at an absurd angle. Having gulped down a handful of aspirin, she manages to crawl out of the wreckage to a nearby cluster of rocks. She hurries, before the adrenaline wears off. She packs cold muddy peat against her leg and ties it in place with the strap of her plane seat. The job of setting her own shattered ankle nearly makes her pass out again, but she keeps her eyes on that hand. She focuses everything on that hand, through the pain and wind. That poor soul in the half-smashed coffin, bruised and purple and bloated like he'd died out in the elements, keeps her together.

Where the hell is she? When she came out of the cloud, there was no river. Clearly she had been pushed off course. That would render the flight plan she logged useless. Help could be a long time coming.

The Little Warrior's back is broken. The tail has cracked off and splintered into dozens of pieces. On impact, one of the wings must have caught the mud, causing the plane to flip. When the tail came off, everything inside scattered to the four winds. She can see debris all around the plane, spread out across the tundra. The first aid kit, the flare gun, her lunch. Gone.

But somehow that coffin stayed. One of the latches held and now it rests on its side, that hand seeming to wave defiantly at Lucy.

She calculates that she was unconscious for only a few hours. It doesn't get fully dark so close to the Arctic Circle, but the sun is low on the horizon. Maybe it's 1:00 or 2:00 a.m. The rain has let up. Now, just wispy clouds hang low over the tundra and the temperature is going up. She won't need a fire and that's a relief.

The Alaska that fascinated Lucy years ago, with its long open stretches and high sky, still manages to soothe her. Even like this, she smells the sweet fireweed and it helps get her breathing, her rhythm, back under control.

She came here only once, part of a mission. When Lucy turned eighteen, her mother sent her to Fairbanks, to a small church early in its establishment. Lucy's job then was to help a group of Filipino immigrants get the mission up and running. But she found God not in the sermons and tedious hymns, but rather in the glaciers, rivers and mountains.

One month after arriving, Lucy caught her first salmon,

alone in a hidden inlet. She gutted the fish on a rock, using a kitchen steak knife, and built a fire with a Zippo lighter, using her socks for kindling. The moment she bit into that fish, she understood she would never leave this place.

Now, as the aspirin begins to wear off and she looks out across the landscape that long ago saved her soul, Lucy realizes it might kill her as well.

Jimmi is furious. A rage he never thought he was capable of feeling swells inside his chest, threatening to cut off his breathing, threatening to explode in violence. He imagines his ax, the motion of the swing, the clean, solid blow required to sink the head deep into his uncle's chest. How surprised his uncle would be. Jimmi imagines Jess's eyes, wide not with pain but with the deep and final understanding of what his nephew is capable of and what is now too late to prevent. That would be his uncle's last thought.

But the rage quickly flames out, leaving a deep, bottomless hole.

"Are you listening to us?" elder Tsosie is saying. "This is very important for you to understand, Jimmi. Pay attention."

Jimmi lifts his eyes toward the council, solely out of a deeply rooted respect. He's heard all he needs to hear. With only forty-eight hours remaining before the hunt, the village council has decided that Jimmi cannot leave, that he has to take care of his uncle instead.

"We know you prepared for this," Tsosie is saying. "We know how much it means to you, but postponing your leaving until next season will not bring any shame on you or your family. Just the opposite."

The full council has come to Jimmi's trailer. All six of them. Some of them so old they stay in their trucks, windows rolled down. Uncle Jess's behavior has spun wildly out of control during the past week. Jimmi has ignored him, uncaring and unconcerned. Whether Jess is doing this on purpose, out of his own inner rage, or truly has no control, Jimmi doesn't care.

His dugout is ready. The season is turning. But Jess will, once again, get the final say. His uncle will once again diminish Jimmi.

"Family comes first, Jimmi," Tsosie is saying. "It's hard, but it is what it is. We can't care for him, and with the men gone, the responsibility falls on you." Jimmi feels the hair on his arms stand up as Tsosie refers to the *men* of the community.

Jess sits in a puddle of mud near the fire pit, his head lolling like a child's. He has a faraway stare now, glazed and without depth. It's like he has shut off.

"I understand, sir."

Tsosie nods and waves off the other council members. "There is no higher calling than helping someone in need, son." He squeezes Jimmi's shoulder weakly before leaving.

Jimmi stands at the foot of his property, watching them drive off into the first swirls of icy rain before he turns to his uncle. Jimmi stands over Jess for a long time, looking down at him, trying to find some fire behind those dead eyes. But there's nothing. Jimmi leaves him there in the cold mud.

It takes less than a day for the bear to come for Lucy.

After a fitful sleep, with tendrils of pain snaking their way up Lucy's thigh every time she moves, morning comes calm and warm. The mosquitoes arrive first, of course, swirling dervishes with no breeze to keep them at bay. By the time she comes fully awake, her hands and face are covered in welts. Tiny streaks of blood drip down her skin from mosquitoes that have drunk so much and so freely they burst before lifting off. She can feel her eyelids become heavy with bumps.

She has no more drugs left, but has to move anyway.

She is slow and sluggish. Her leg burns, she expected

that. But her stomach is queasy and her forehead throbs. She coughs, and a thin watery streak of bloody phlegm appears. There's something wrong inside, something else that's broken beside her ankle. Lucy suddenly feels thirsty, deeply, uncontrollably thirsty.

She presses her hands, palms up, into the muddy tundra and they slowly fill with filthy water. Without thinking, she lifts the mud to her mouth, but gags almost immediately and is unable to keep it down.

Lucy is able to lie on her stomach and turn her body back toward the plane. On her elbows, she begins to drag through the soft earth. Her leg gets snagged in the viney wildflowers often, but she blots out the oppressive pain. She focuses on that hand, now a deep shade of blue and buzzing with flies. She forces her thoughts back to her little cabin in Koyukuk, the home she's made for herself here, among the natives who took so long to regard her with anything but suspicion, this petite half-American with dyed red hair and no husband. She built her own home and attended village ceremonies and learned the names of the tribe. She was never one of them, but she became something approaching an accepted curiosity. And when she began to fly, when the *Little Warrior* became the conduit that connected her community with the rest of the Yukon Valley, the elders relaxed, stopped thinking about what she wanted from them and began considering how she could help.

She reaches the cockpit and begins to tear at the seat cover. There's not much left of her precious girl. It takes a while to get enough fabric to fashion a crude head cover. She wraps her hands as well as she can.

And then, while she rests there against the plane's broken fuselage, two things happen at once. She realizes how warm the tundra has become, the heat rising in tiny tendrils up from the mud. The humidity suddenly becomes stifling. From her own sweat and blood, or from the rot that has set in from the corpse in the back of her plane, the stench has become oppressive.

She realizes there are crows circling high above her wreck, and as the meaning of these developments begins to sink into her pain-shocked mind, she hears an unmistakable grunt, deep and low.

Lucy squints her eyes through blood streaks and blurring vision to the horizon. A light brown fuzzy creature is approaching, its gait unmistakable.

"Oh God," she says to the air.

Jimmi looks down at the men loading their boats. He sits on a rise, just over the river. From up here he can look east toward the river and over the vast tundra. Behind him, to the west, his small town and its tiny airport butt up against the mountain range. The *Little Warrior*, painted bright red, is unmistakable against the dirt runway.

He can see his trailer from here. Jess has not left the ragged old sofa in front of the TV for days. Jimmi's uncle hasn't spoken a word since the elders left. Maybe he never will again.

The boy turns his attention back to the boats. Most of the gear is brought down to the river on horses, or crude sleds that the men, sometimes with their families, pull to the river. Those sleds go right into the boats, as the men will use them to haul their game when the snows come.

The only other sixteen-year-old hunter, Rohan, is lashing his pack into the front of the canoe. It will be the first time Rohan is out on his own, and Jimmi watches as Rohan's father clasps hands with his son and pulls him into a hug. They stay that way for a long time, before silently pushing off and heading up river.

Jimmi sits up there on that rise until all the canoes are gone, the women and children have retreated back to the village and night falls. He waits for the moon, then slinks down to the shore. He has no intention of going home ever again.

He walks along the shore for a ways, downstream, away from where the men headed. He's stashed his dugout in a clump of brush and rocks. He has no gear, no supplies, no food. He won't need any.

By the light of the half moon, he pushes off and lets the current do the work. The early melt coming off the glaciers gives the water a silvery glow, and the river is high. He doesn't know where he's headed, exactly. The river will eventually feed out to the Bering Sea, but he'd never get that far even if he wanted to. The river will decide for him.

After a while, Jimmi begins to feel the rhythm of the water as it ebbs and flows around pocket islands and inlets. The night is clear but cold, and the smell of a coming storm hangs in the air.

The canoe is pulled around a blind turn and Jimmi is suddenly aware of a form on the shore. The grizzly looks up as Jimmi passes. Perhaps twenty yards separate the two, passing in the night. Jimmi gently pulls his oar from the water and watches quietly. The bear swings its head back and forth, an early territorial warning, but even in the darkness both creatures understand that the other means no harm. Soon, the bear moves away, its heavy dark form disappearing into the night.

This is the place, Jimmi thinks, that was the sign.

He allows the current to do as it will, to take him to his final place. After a few minutes, without anyone steering, the canoe grounds on a high gravel bar. Jimmi pulls it up and walks silently into the tundra, into the darkness, far enough to be out of sight, but not out of hearing of the river.

He strips off his denim jeans and jacket, pulls off his gloves and hat and lays them at his feet. Then he sits on the frosty wildflowers, the cool edges feeling like tiny ice cubes against his skin. The temperature will drop tonight, perhaps enough, perhaps not.

But Jimmi will wait. He'll wait there, naked on the land, until his body is no longer able to function, or until some animal becomes curious about the stock-still human sitting in the grass. He closes his eyes and feels a slight shiver and begins to consider the end.

The bear takes its time. With nothing to scare it off, and the smell of rotting meat and blood in the air, Lucy understands she has nowhere to run and no way to escape. Normally, the bears won't eat dead flesh. But if this one is hungry and Lucy can give the bear what it wants, that might make a difference.

"I'm sorry, I'm sorry," she says over and over as she desperately claws at the corner of the casket, popping the nails, her fingers turning raw with the effort. "Please forgive me, I'm sorry."

She focuses, saving her energy for the creature if it comes in too fast or doesn't wait for her to finish. All her movement is keeping it at bay, for now, but that smell is too powerful.

The side of the casket falls free with a screechy pop, and Lucy turns away as a swarm of flies fills what's left of the *Little Warrior*. There's no cremation and no formaldehyde in Ahtna death rituals. The corpse would have been in the ground by now. Lucy stifles the urge to gag, grabs two handfuls of the body's clothes and heaves. She can't stand on her own feet, so the leverage is poor and for a terrifying moment it appears the body will roll out and onto Lucy. But she drags herself away and manages, on her hands and knees, to pull the body out into the open, away from the plane.

She can see the creature, not fifty yards from the plane, its huge brown head low to the ground. The bear is breathing hard, each breath kicking up flecks of dust and dirt. It wants to charge. It wants to eat.

"Come on," Lucy says to the body, still staring at the bear. "Help me out here."

She's able to drag the body, but slowly. It keeps getting tangled in low brush and mud. She wants to get the body as far from the plane as she can, then use the fuselage as refuge, the only thing she has.

But the bear has had enough. It snorts, a low deep growl, and begins to viciously paw the ground. "No, no bear! she shouts, waving her hands, trying to seem bigger.

The bear charges.

"Oh, shit, shit!" Lucy drags herself hard, half standing, the pain in her leg roars through her pelvis and stomach, but adrenaline keeps her moving. She gets only ten feet from the body before the bear is on it, biting down hard into the neck of the corpse.

Lucy turns away, concentrates on putting distance between the bear's meal and herself. She can hear the tearing of flesh, the bear growling as it bites and chews, its long territorial breaths.

She reaches the plane and succumbs to the pain. With tears streaming down her face and a bear feasting on the corpse only yards away, Lucy slumps down into the mud, only half-conscious. She's done. If the corpse isn't enough, the bear will come for her next.

Lucy sits there watching. Bits of blood and flesh speckle the bear's snout and face. "She's beautiful," Lucy says out loud.

Then, in the moments she believes to be her last, with the growl of the bear in her ears and pain shooting through her body like a thousand needles, Lucy hears a loud clap, like a distant thunderstorm. The sound seems to rattle the aluminum of the *Little Warrior*. The bear lets out an angry howl, turns away from the corpse and flees. Through her tears Lucy watches in amazement as the creature runs from the plane, its brown fur rippling in the wind.

And in the final moments before she closes her eyes, she thinks she sees a figure, rifle in hand, running toward the crash. Then, darkness.

Jimmi looks down at what remains of his uncle Jess's bloated and blue body, now torn into ragged, meaty pieces. Some of it—a hand, part of a thigh—is gone altogether. Food for the bear.

Jess's face is mostly there, a section of his cheek sliding down from the cheekbone, but mostly recognizable. Jimmi looks down, impassive and unfeeling. He searches for some emotional reaction to what he sees, but there's nothing. Jess is back to the earth.

The land did not kill Jimmi. He sat out on the tundra for three days, cold, shivering, despondent. But not dying. On the third day of his fast, he opened his eyes, stood up and paddled back to his village.

And when he returned to his trailer to find his uncle slumped over the kitchen table, the side of his face blood-thick in a pool of spilled alcohol, he believed his purification to be final, his responsibility to his family and his tribe to be over. He refused to perform final rites, refused to open his home to the village burial ceremony or to well-wishers. He declined to walk his uncle's simple casket out to the *Little Warrior*, did not even watch as Lucy's plane set off into a storm to carry the coffin south to the tribe's original land near the bay.

But when the plane disappeared, something inside him snapped. His resolve was replaced by guilt. Perhaps had he been there he could have saved his uncle. Perhaps. He cried for his lost parents, his lost history and his nearly lost life. He instantly regretted his actions. So, just an hour after he got word, he vowed to make things right. He would find his uncle and bury him properly. He'd put the old man into the ground himself if he had to, and that meant finding the plane.

Jimmi was the first out of town when news of the plane's disappearance began to circulate. His canoe was in the water even as the storm raged, even as rescue party plans were being formulated. He didn't have any interest in waiting.

He'd been tracking the *Little Warrior* for miles, first following the river, then tracing the storm track. Then a lucky break when he found a bit of glass near the shore, some paper and fabric. Then a sharp smell, like rotting flesh, to the east.

He crested a rise near the pieces, just a half mile from the water, and saw the pack of ravens circling on the horizon. He broke into a run.

And now it is clear that this will be Jess's final resting place. Jimmi will dig as far into the tundra as he can, up to the permafrost. The boy will bring his family's history to an end, here.

"Is someone there?" A weak, hoarse voice drifts over from the plane wreck.

Lucy! Jimmi slings his rifle, grabs his pack and trots over to the wreck, where he finds Lucy. She's nearly blind with loss of blood and dehydration. Jimmi kneels in the muck, lifts her head gently, and gingerly brings his canteen against her lips.

"You're going to be okay," he whispers.

Lucy pulls hard on the water and feels the liquid run down her cheeks and she begins to cry. She feels Jimmi's hands under her neck, her head.

"Jimmi, is that you? Can you help me?"

"Yes, of course I can," Jimmi says. "I can help you."

Gold Dust

"THAT'S THE DAMNEDEST THING," I mutter to the dust.

The corner post is split down the middle like somebody cut it in half for firewood. I look stupidly at it for a couple minutes, trying to figure out what happened. The post is now a shoulder-high V, the barb unrolled in some spots, busted in others. The split's big enough to walk through, easy, and that's exactly what half a dozen head did.

I wipe my forehead with the back of my sleeve—Goddamned hot day already, and barely even dawn. Well, there's no getting around it.

Getting down off Junior takes me a while. Poor guy's back sags almost as bad as mine, I guess, but he doesn't care. He just stands there, rock still, until I'm able to swing free and drop gingerly to the dirt. I pat his hind and a cloud of white dust billows off his brown coat, leaving a hand mark like he's been rolled in flour.

No need to tie him down. Neither Junior nor I move fast anymore. He just stands still in the dust, watching me, swishing flies with his tail every so often, but even the bugs seem lazy in this heat.

I stretch. Getting out to the northwest corner took nearly an hour. When Frank Barnes let me know some of my cattle were wandering on his property, I figured I'd start my circuit nearest where they were found. I'm relieved to not have to ride the whole damn 10,000-acre property.

It was good of Frank to call and let me know. Those new phone lines might look ugly as sin, but they make it unnecessary to ride the half dozen miles between our houses anymore.

Anyway, others might just slaughter the lost cows as soon as they were found, add to their bottom line and nobody would be any wiser. I've known it to happen. Frank's different, though.

The post can't be salvaged. No cow did this, that's for sure. And Frank wouldn't have told me about it if he did it, and what would the point of that be anyway?

I look around. The nearest dirt road is five miles away. The dirt and grass and scrub extend to the horizon. There are no footprints that I can see. Maybe lightning hit it.

I pull the pliers out of my back pocket and clip the remaining barb off the two post halves. That gives me enough extra to at least spindle the two pieces of post back together. That will do for now. The post hole is still deep enough to hold and I'm able to shove the post's end back in and shore it up with some rocks and left-over splinters before packing in some sand and dirt. My back aches after a time, and I need to stand up.

That's when I see him—two, maybe more, miles off, coming up out of Mad River Gulch. Seems like a fresh horse, but he's too far away to really tell. The silhouette of the horse and rider shivers and shakes in the fog of heat rising off the prairie, and with the sun at my back all I can make out is a black figure.

Down on the other side of the gulch, there's a whole line of oil derricks owned by South Dakota. Could be a state inspector, maybe not. The rider is heading toward me, though.

It'll be a while till he gets here, so I pull a small spool of barb out of my saddle bag and start tying the broken ends back on to the temporary corner post. I string the wire around the post a few times but don't bother snapping any off. I'll have to come back out to replace the post anyway, so it's easier to just keep it all together for now.

Takes me a good half hour to get the job right, and when I return to Junior I can see the rider's only a hundred yards out now. He's moving pretty quick—seems like a young man, thirties, maybe more, black coat, not so dusty, though. Fine horse, white with gray and black spots.

I make a show out of fixing my saddle bag and slowly turn Junior to stand between me and the rider. I slip my Colt out of the bag and slide it under my belt behind my back.

Then I wait, shifting my weight from knee to creaky knee. I can finally really see him when he gets about twenty-five yards away. He's young, has a dark complexion, no whiskers—not wearing a hat. His hair is slicked back, like he's got grease in it. He's not accustomed to his horse. He wants to ride hard, but it's easy to see he don't sit well in a brand new saddle. He's not wearing gloves. Dumb. His hands are red and chapped.

When he gets close enough to talk I touch my brim. "Morning," I say, nice and easy. I'm looking right at the sun, and have to squint hard to make him out.

"Good morning, sir," he says. "Doing some mending this morning?"

I spit and nod. "What can I do for you, son?"

"Well sir, I represent some folks who thought they ought to introduce themselves to you." His voice is high, and he speaks fast like his tongue is having trouble keeping up with his thoughts. I don't see any weapon, and he's wearing some kind of shoes under his dungarees. He runs the tips of his fingers over his tongue, and pushes back his dusty hair.

I prod Junior to move just a bit to the left so I'm able to see the kid better. He doesn't seem to notice what I'm doing.

"Folks sent you, huh?" I say.

His laugh is nervous. I tense up as the kid sits up on the saddle and reaches down into a small black side bag. When he looks back up I have my gun trained on the center of his chest. "Nice and easy now, friend," I say. "Move your hand out of that bag slow."

His expression changes fast, and he narrows his eyes. "You've got it all wrong, sir," he says quietly. He keeps his eyes on mine, not on my gun, a sign that he's been in this situation before. "Fine gun, sir. The Great Equalizer. Been a while since I saw one."

"My granddaddy's," I say. "It works just fine."

He moves his hand up out of the bag slowly and produces an envelope. "I'm just here for an introduction." He tosses the envelope on the ground at my feet and raise his hands, palms up, toward me. "Just a letter, sir, no need for violence."

I lower the gun, but rest it on Junior's saddle, where the kid can see. He lowers his hands.

"Times are changing, sir." He speaks slowly now, deliberately. "They are carving out that mountain, down there in Rapid City, just thirty miles south of here. People are going to come to see it."

I keep my mouth shut and it seems to frustrate him.

"They are going to build roads and places where families can stay, and this land is going to become much more than dirt and sage," he says. "You're not going to be able to manage it all by yourself."

"'Cause I'm old, son?"

A long silence falls between us, and I spit again just for show.

"I'll take my leave, sir." He backs his horse off but, before turning, says, "A lot of bad can happen to this land, sir, things much worse than a busted fence post."

Without another word, he gallops off, leaving a white trail of dust for me to contemplate.

Frank's place is an old girl, built well before South Dakota was South Dakota. My neighbor's been working his front porch since the Civil War, it seems, and that's what he's doing when I ride up. Takes me most of the morning to get here, but I know I'm welcome even when he's out on the property. I'm glad he's here, though.

"Frank," I say from my perch on Junior, "I think we might have a problem."

Frank Barnes is a tall man, built like one of his tractors, hard as one too. His land's been in his family longer than anyone in the county, 'cept the Indians of course. When Marta and I decided to buy, he sold us our plot.

"You talking about that city kid, one with the fancy horse?"

"I think he might be the one who busted up my post, Frank," I say.

Frank gives this a long thought, hammer in hand swinging by his side. "Well, come on down then, you'll stay here tonight."

I tie off Junior and follow Frank in. Even though I've been at his place more times than I can count, it always seems new. Frank is always fiddling with something, a new sink, new roof, furniture. Today I'm amazed to discover a beautiful rug, thick and intricate with red and yellow diamond designs.

"Native?" I ask. "Cheyenne?"

Frank shakes his head. "A gift. Have a seat, Jake."

The one constant in Frank's house has been his rocking chair, and I collapse into it like a sack of potatoes. It had been a long morning. A poof of white dust billows up around my seat and sinks onto the new rug.

"Sorry Frank, been riding all day."

He smiles and hands me a tin of steaming coffee and I swear it's never tasted better. He sits down across from me in a well-worn sofa.

Frank takes a deep breath. "I asked them to come, Jake. I'm sorry."

For a moment, I miss who he's referring to. "You . . . what?"

"City kid with the fancy horse. His name's Daniel. They're from Los Angeles. I'm selling, Jake, I can't do this anymore."

My heart sinks, and for the first time in many years—through sickness, and Marta dying, and dust storms—I feel real fear. I make a calm show of it, though, something Frank himself taught me. "Can't do what, Frank?"

"We're old men, Jake. Wives gone, nothing but dirt to show. Look at you, you're covered in chalk. I got a kid in Austin, doing ok, figured I'd head down there and disappear for a while. Maybe forever."

"This is your life, Frank, your only life."

He leans back and rubs his eyes. "Don't have to be, Jake. Things change. You were a teacher before all this. Why don't you—"

I cut him off. "You sold us out! To mobsters from L.A.? You did this?"

"It has nothing to do with you, Jake. I had no idea they'd come around for you too. And they ain't no mobsters."

"They cleaved my fence, Frank! Read this!" I flip the letter onto his lap. "It says that the *pleasure* of my company is requested in Rapid City. It says that if I sell within two weeks, I'll be put up in some new fangled old folks hotel in the city. It says I'll be rich and happy the rest of my life, Frank! Breaking my property, then telling me I'll be rich?"

"They are serious men, Jake," Frank says. "But it don't matter because if not them then somebody else will be coming. There's roads coming, Jake. We got nothing here anymore anybody wants except to make roads and hotels on. How much happiness does your cattle bring you, Jake? Ain't you tired of eatin' dust?"

I am tired of it, but after thirty-two years you get used to it, it becomes who you are. Frank has done it even longer.

"How much?" I ask him.

"What do you mean, Jake?".

"Don't be stupid, Frank. How much are they giving you?"

Frank is quiet for a long time and I let him be. "Enough to make it worth it, Jake. More than I could ever have imagined."

"And now they are here. What happens if I don't sell, Frank?"

"I'm sure—" he pauses. "Why wouldn't you, Jake?"

I take a while to get up out of that damn rocker, but I have nothing left to say and a long ride home. I leave without saying goodbye.

Long ago, in what seems to have been another life altogether, Marta and I called Rapid City home. The town was sleepy then, the streets muddy. There were no tourists, there was nothing a tourist would want to see. Everything is different now.

The trip takes Junior and me a couple days to make it down, but the weather holds and it feels good to have such a destination in mind. Even Junior seems to perk up a little knowing he's going to the city.

We amble down Main Street, a busy jumble of buggies, horses and now autos all fighting for real estate. The Gold Dust Redevelopment Company rents a small storefront, a hat shop on one side and an Italian restaurant on the other. There are no hitching posts anymore, so I tie Junior to a lamppost and walk right in.

This isn't an office. A few young men sit around a round table playing cards and smoking. They all look up when I walk in, and don't seem to care much about me one way or the other until I pull my long coat aside enough to reveal my holster. Then all of a sudden I'm the center of attention.

They all kick back from the table like I got the plague and make a big show of displaying their various weapons.

"What do you need, old-timer?" the leader of the group says. He's a big fellow, yellow hair, meaty hands.

"That a Luger, son?" I nod my head toward the gun sticking out of his pants. "You German? I thought all you mobsters were Wops."

There's a long pause, during which I'm sure some of them are wondering where they would dump my body. Then the German starts laughing and pretty soon they're all cackling and pounding on the table and holding their sides. I start laughing too, I figure it's best if I do.

"You're OK, old man! Come on over here and sit in with us!"

And so I'm invited to a real live mobster card game. They're not a bad bunch of fellows, really; out of their element, perhaps, here in the dust and hills. But we play and I learn.

They tell me about Daniel Riggio, the one who visited me. They boys call him "Legs" but I don't ask why. There are real estate players from all over the country coming to the Dakotas. Frank was wrong about them. This group was sent by an outfit out of Las Vegas, of all places, a casino owner who runs a place called The Gold Dust. It's not just Frank and me. The boys tell me they already have bought up thousands of acres, north and south of Rapid City.

"You should see that thing," the German, whom the boys call "Fritz," says to me. "Rushmore, that's the name of it. We got a hunk of land just west of that mountain. Gonna put a hotel there, maybe a junk shop with photo books and sell hamburgers. Who knows? Lots of potential."

I kind of admire them. Aside from the violence and scare tactics, maybe they have a point. At least they're working for a living.

The front door slams open and Daniel strides in. When he sees me sitting at the table, he freezes. "Fritz!" It's not a question.

"He just showed up, boss. Just playing some cards is all," Fritz says, eyes down.

"Get out, all of you," Daniel says to the boys. He's pretty angry, but I chuckle a little. He's wearing some kind of phony cowboy suit, the sort Roy Rogers might wear, with tassels.

"Settle down, son," I say. "You don't want to muss up that pretty hair of yours." He turns beet red and comes at me, but doesn't get three steps before my revolver is once again beaded on his chest. The boys are gone, it's only me and Daniel. "Easy, son, or I'll end this right here."

He holds up his hands and takes a deep breath. "You are a surprise, Mr. James." He shakes his head, then laughs himself. "I apologize. Where are my manners? It's a pleasure to meet you formally." He extends his hand.

I lower the gun and we shake.

"That's the second time your Dragoon has been pointed at me, sir. It's a fine weapon, but the Wild West is ages past."

"I suppose it is, Daniel."

We stand there for a few minutes, and my hip starts to bother me but I hold my ground.

"You know why we're here?" he asks.

"I do."

"Are you willing to negotiate for your land?"

"I am not."

Another long silence follows.

"And Daniel," I say, "this here is a Walker, not a Dragoon."

He lifts one eyebrow and the tension in the room seems to drain. "Your granddad was a Texas Ranger?"

I nod.

"Will you walk with me, Mr. James? I'd like to show you something."

We stroll through town on foot toward the long ridge that separates Main Street from the mountains. I move slow, but Daniel seems to be enjoying the day and he adjusts to move at my speed.

We wind our way up the rutty footpath toward what appear

to be smooth gray rock formations along the ridge. The day is warm, but a southern breeze floats out of the Black Hills, making the walk pleasant. It's a fine day, and there's movement all around.

As we climb higher above the city, Daniel points out landmarks. To the north, the wide sweep of Rapid Creek cuts through town and ducks behind several brick row houses. Near the center of town, a towering marble and stone building shoots straight up out of an empty lot. One four-story turret is already finished. The other half of the building appears from here to be crawling with ants—workers scrambling over scaffolding.

Daniel catches my gaze. "City library, Mr. James. The largest in the state, even bigger than Pierre's from what I understand."

I begin to feel a sense of calm. I haven't strolled through Rapid City, or any city, for many years and I'm surprised by how much it's grown.

"There, can you see it?" Daniel is pointing to the ridge, now only about fifty yards away.

"What the? Is that—?"

"A dinosaur!" Daniel claps his hands, and for a moment he is a child. I look into his eyes and there is something else there different from the hair treatment and the shoes and the menace. "WPA. City is having it built."

I'm an old man and I've seen a lot of things. But I've never seen concrete dinosaurs. The ridge is full of them, huge, fifteen or twenty feet high, every one of them a dark metal gray. We reach the ridge and I'm out of breath so I sit down on the stony tail of a large hump-backed creature with a long neck like a giraffe and I just stare.

Daniel slides on a pair of silver sunglasses and squints up at the beast. "This one is something called a Brontosaurus. God-damn big, huh?"

"How do you know that?" I ask.

He laughs and claps a big meaty hand on my shoulder. "Because I love it here, Mr. James. Rapid City, I mean."

I keep quiet.

"Look, Mr. James, do you know why the city is building these stupid concrete things? I mean it's a works admin project, right? Why not a post office or whatever?" He doesn't let me answer. "Tourists! Just up the road they are expanding the airport. No kidding. People are already driving halfway across the country to go see a half-carved-out George Washington's nose. Can you believe that?"

I look down the ridge at Rapid City, its dirt streets and gleaming ironwork banks and the shimmer of fancy cars rolling slowly down its main streets.

"Everything here is going to be different, Mr. James. Hell, it already is," he says.

"By different you mean more valuable, right?"

The smile drains from his face. "Why do you say that, Mr. James? Why make me seem like some greedy son of a bitch? I worked hard to get where I am and I'm trying to help you out here, to help you see how good the rest of your life could be."

"Can I see my land from here, Daniel?" I ask.

He looks north over the city for a time, then shakes his head. "I couldn't say for sure, sir. Not a lot to go on, just mostly flat prairie land."

"Give me a hand up, son." He helps me to my feet and I hang on to his elbow with one hand and begin a sweep from the west with the other. "Right there, follow my finger, that's Bandit Gulch, a dry river bed that used to drain all the way to Colorado, back when these boys here were more than concrete. About thirteen miles east of the gulch is Thunder Butte. Can you see it? Follow the horizon for about two fist lengths and right up there, it's only a dot, that's White Butte, the highest point in North Dakota. That's 150 miles from here, Daniel."

He's not looking at the horizon anymore. He's looking at

me. I continue. "And right there, just west of that grassland—that's called Eldorado Seam—that's my land. I can follow it all the way down to the eastern border, to where you busted my fence."

He jerks his arm away and is back to his old self again. "Why are you telling me this?" he asks.

"Because I love it here, too, Daniel. It's all I have left."

We stand there for what seems like a long time.

"I should get back," he finally says, and stomps off down toward the street, leaving me to navigate the walk back by myself.

The days go by quickly. I get supplies before leaving Rapid City, and take my time on the ride back home. Junior moves so slow it sometimes feels like we're not moving at all, but that's fine. I make camp in the dust and the sage, or stamp out some nice prairie grass if we can find it.

On the second night, we stop near a half rotted away butte, the soil chalky from the salt drain. We make bed atop the thing and I sit back against my saddle and watch the sun set and the sky roll up in a big orange and red wave and it reminds me of some of the first rides Marta and I took around our property.

On the third night, I make a detour down into the drainage behind the house to the family plot. Of course, it's only Marta and a bunch of goats, two dogs and five cats down there. Don't remember any of their names, the pets I mean. This is a pretty place. Marta picked it out herself on one of our tours. Her grave sits at the end of a long rocky swoop, her feet pointing north toward the border. Little grassy embankments on either side provide a nice little sitting space. I suppose if water ever flowed back into this mini-ravine, Marta would be underwater, but she might like that too.

I sleep on that little buffer that night, Junior on one side, Marta on the other. I'm at peace and I feel like my life has had meaning. There's a little rain and off in the distance lightning flashes and the evening feels final and comforting.

Back at the ranch I take inventory. I'm not sure exactly how long it will be before they come, but I am sure they will come. I unload my supplies and take the time to sweep up and clean house. I never was real good at that sort of thing and after a couple hours it feels pointless.

They come on the morning of my second day home, exactly one week after my stroll with Daniel.

They pull up my drive in a fine new sedan. Daniel is in the back seat and he gets out along with three other fellas. The driver is the German boy. He stays in the idling car. They are all wearing suits and sunglasses.

I step out onto my porch and lean on a post.

"Morning, Daniel," I say.

The boys with him snicker at my using his formal name, but he doesn't let it bother him.

"It's time to go, Mr. James," Daniel says. He takes off his sunglasses. They stand there, dust whipping around from a prairie wind, their black suits turning white. Maybe the kid thinks it's Wild West time.

Not today. "I'm sorry Daniel, I wish I could make this easier for you." I say.

His shoulders sag and I feel sorry for him for a passing moment. "There's a whole new chapter waiting for you, Mr. James." He's whining a little.

"And do what, Daniel?" I ask. "Play cards in some rooming house I suppose? Doesn't sound very interesting."

"I don't want this to be hard, Jake." he says.

"Me either, son." I sigh. "Would you do me a favor?"

"What's that?"

"Take care of Junior for me," I say.

He looks down. "Mr. James, really, I don't—"

"Daniel!" I bark at him and he looks up fast, like he's been slapped. "Take care of it, and make it fast and painless. Would you do that for me?"

"Yes, sir," he says quietly.

"Give me a minute." I step back inside, but there's nothing there for me. I slide a picture of Marta into my shirt pocket.

Daniel is waiting for me when I come out. "Give me a hand here, kid," I say.

I come down the porch, steadying myself on his shoulder. I stand there a moment, and the wind plays at our backs, and Daniel waits for me to be ready.

I reach around to the back of my trousers and pull the Colt. Daniel steps back fast and the boys near the car scramble a bit, but I raise my other hand to show it's OK.

I lay the gun across my outstretched palm and offer it to Daniel. He pauses a moment, seems about to say something, but doesn't. He reaches out, takes the gun, and holds it awkwardly at his side.

"Good luck, Daniel," I say.

"You too, Mr. James."

We shake, and I make my way to the Sedan. Fritz opens the door for me and one of the boys helps me into the back.

Daniel says a few words to Fritz, and the boys get in on both sides of me, and we begin the slow ride back to Rapid City.

"You'll come play cards with us, Mr. James," Fritz says. It's not a question.

"Sure, Fritz," I say.

I turn and gaze out the back window and see Daniel looking up at my home, the Colt hanging loosely in one hand and a clipboard in the other. And the dust swirls up and clouds my view and there's no longer anything to see.

By Hammer and Hand

I AM AN ASTRONAUT. I am a poet. I am a chemical engineer.

I will work on the sharpest of deadlines. I will write till my fingers bleed. I will research anything for you until my eyes burn and the coffee no longer keeps me awake.

Last year, I earned $87,000. Legally. In the process, I learned how to extract marrow from the exoskeleton of a Pacific sand shrimp. I discovered the symbolic nature of water in the Book of John. And I plotted the air speed velocity of a Piper PA-32 against the often unpredictable wind shear found in Denali National Park.

I am a fisherman. I am a theologian. I am a pilot.

My desktop dings. An email from a particularly impatient student appears.

RUNING OUT OF TIME! PAPER DUE FRI 10:00 A.M. HAVE NOT HERD FROM YOU REGARD STATUS. PLEASE CONFIRM!

I hit delete. I have no time for such wavering. I'm best when pressed. Deadlines are when I really hit my stride. Besides, her commission (that's what we call it here) is an easy one, a paper I've written a dozen times before: three pages on the relationship between Virgil and Dante. I can write it by heart. They do not ask much of college freshmen these days.

I will write it Thursday afternoon in a burst of speed, like a pitcher zeroing in on the strike zone. My company asks for $100 per page. I get half. That's $150 for an hour of work.

30

I am a scholar. I am an athlete. I am an investor.

My desk is like an air traffic tower control panel. I know where everything is, I have everything I need, I can be anything that's needed.

"Sam!" My boss strides through the bullpen (that's the terminal area where I work with sixteen other technicians) like a matador. I look up from my desktop pallet. "I'm getting a shit-storm of emails from some little fucktwit in Jersey City about Dante. You on this?"

"It's done, Barry." I lie, but who cares. He is an idiot. "It's done, but our agreement calls for three to six days. If I send her a copy before that it'll set a precedent, and we're all going to be working twenty-four hours for the brats. Do you want that, Barry?"

"Well, no, but I—"

"Just ignore it. Is that all you need? Because I have a geometry paper I need to finish."

Barry skulks off, leaving a whiff of pepperoni and Old Spice floating in my cubicle. I wave the air furiously and go back to my crossword.

I am the boss. I am the boss. I am the boss.

I seldom think about the generation that will soon be running the country, the state and this town; not because of some ethical hiccup or even out of pity. Rather, it is just not worth it to care. Nobody actually cares about this, about everyday life. We are just blips in the bigger picture, hardly noticeable at all.

Let me ask you this: What is the more important accomplishment, walking on the moon or *American Idol*? The answer is that neither matters. Just make a few bucks, buy yourself a cookie and get some sleep.

I am a philosopher. I am a nihilist. I am aware.

Down past the rows of cubes and around the corner from the water cooler, in an afterthought of a break room, there is a poster of a runner climbing bleachers at a stadium. The poster reads, "Without preparation, there can be no achievement." I do not use the break room because I do not need breaks, but I go there sometimes to consider this poster. An argument can be made that those students who use our service are being resourceful. After all, if not from us, they would likely just plagiarize from Wiki. At least I give them original work, something they can be proud of.

I often wish I could keep track of the grades I give them. There is no refund if they fail the class, but I do not fail. I never fail.

I am an artist. I am unique. I am original.

Later in the week, one day before the Dante deadline, there is a commotion from someplace out of my line of sight. I pay no attention. I am engrossed in an article on Hephaestus, the blacksmith of the gods. It amuses me to discover that his forge was a volcano. The research is not for any commission specifically, but I like to keep on top of things.

Suddenly, I am confronted by a red-headed teenager with a knife. I'm momentarily put off sorts.

"You," she yells, "you're the one who's writing my paper, you're ignoring me!" People are standing up from their cubes. I hope someone has dialed 911.

"How did you get in here?" I ask. I surprise myself by sounding calm, and that fact actually helps to calm me. I glance over at Barry but that fat ass is just standing in his office, watching. I swear he's grinning.

"It don't matter," she says, half crying. "I need to pass that class! You don't understand!"

The knife appears to be some kind of cutlery, maybe a steak knife. Her hands are shaking.

"I do understand," I say evenly, "very much so. It's the Dante paper, isn't it? The paper will be beautiful. You'll be very happy."

She hesitates. Several of my braver cube mates have moved closer. Most have fled.

"It's just—I can't get anything right, you know?" She lowers her hand and I move toward her. She sees me coming and sloppily thrusts the knife at me. I pull back my pelvis and use an x-block to twist away her captured wrist. The knife flies out of her hand, and I finish the move by pulling her arm around and bringing her to the floor with a knee to her back.

She is crying and shouting and a couple of guys who came up from accounting grab her and drag her off. I put the knife in a lunch bag, figuring maybe the police will want it. As I go back to my article, everybody is watching me, including Barry, but I ignore them.

I am a martial artist. I am a negotiator. I am unfaltering.

Afternoon Television

THE TOAST WAS BURNT, again, for the third time in a week. Traci waved away the tiny puffs of smoke coming from the toaster so as not to set off the smoke alarm. She wasn't sure if the smoke alarm had batteries, but she didn't want to take the chance.

She could get distracted sometimes. There were so many things to watch on television in the morning; game shows, sunny talk shows, even cartoons sometimes. And in the afternoon, when Herb went to work and Traci had the apartment to herself, it was a whole new world. The soaps did nothing for her, but Mona and Gerry and Betty Lynn brought interesting people right into Traci's kitchen.

She absently scraped the black flakes off the toast and smeared the slices generously with jelly so Herb wouldn't notice. The shower shut off in the bathroom and the kitchen pipes rattled. This was something Traci couldn't figure out. Herb had tried to explain that in an apartment as small as theirs, all the pipes were connected to one another. Every time anybody used any faucet, the whole place rattled. No matter. Plumbing was Herb's concern.

Traci set out a plate for herself, though she was on a diet. She poured two glasses of orange juice and turned up the television. The weather report was coming on and she knew Herb would want to hear it before he left for work. She was pleased with the way she had rearranged Herb's kitchen when she moved in. Herb let her, of course. He called it Traci's territory. She had found that by moving the table out into the center of the tiny kitchen, she could put the small black and white television on top of the fridge and they could watch while they ate. Breakfast was close to a ritual now and Traci was proud of that.

It wasn't like Herb was a slob or anything. Traci figured his first wife had broken him of that habit. Traci was just used to having a lot of control around her old house. Before moving in with Herb she had lived as an only child, with her divorced father. This gave her lots of opportunity to be the woman of the house. That always had a nice ring to it. She was now the woman in Herb's house.

She heard a floorboard squeak behind her, but didn't have the time to get up out of her chair before Herb's hands were on her shoulders.

"Morning, doll," he said. He smelled fresh and soapy and his hands were still cool from the water. "How's my cheerleader?"

She smiled. All through high school, even last year, her final year at Cleardale, she had tried out for the cheerleading squad. She never even came close. Her weight always held her back. All those anemic momma's girls made Traci sick. She tried out anyway, every year, to the taunts and jeers of her classmates. Herb had been the first person to listen, really listen, when she told this story. And now she was his cheerleader and glad to be.

His fingers pressed deeply into her shoulders and neck and she felt her muscles loosening pleasantly. "I put together some breakfast, hon," she said.

"Uh-hmm."

His hands didn't let up, though, and she noticed he still wore only his bath towel. She leaned back and rested her head on his bare belly. His hands slid down, over her breasts.

They made love right there, on the table, with her fanny turning red and sticky from the toast and jelly. The orange juice spilled. Herb's grunting eventually mixed with the manic forecasting of the morning weatherman and finally all sounds disappeared and Traci could only hear her heartbeat.

After, Herb helped her clean up. They didn't say much, but Traci was still feeling tingly and lightheaded. "You're going to be late for work," she said. "I'll finish up here."

"Sure?"

She nodded.

"Is something wrong?"

She opened her mouth to say no, but closed it.

"It's the show tomorrow, isn't it? You're worried."

"Yeah."

"We can cancel. Even this late, we don't have to go."

"I want to. I want to let everyone know."

"Okay. Good. I'm proud of you."

He gave her a quick peck on the cheek and was out the door.

* * *

The past few days had gone by in a blur. Last Saturday, at the Thruway Mall, Traci had paused for a quick taco snack at the food court, when the young man in the fancy suit had approached her. At first, she thought he was one of those mall survey guys, the ones that ask you the silly questions about God-knows-what. But he had quickly put that idea to rest when he handed her his card.

Len Spinkle—Mona Day Productions

"Mona Day?" Traci whispered.

"Yes, ma'am. Do you know who Mona Day is?"

He had Traci's full attention now. "Do I know?! Are you kidding? I watch her every day practically. God, she's so nice. Like the time when she had those twins on the show, you know the one was a nun and the other a transves—"

"Yes, that's super," Len politely cut her off. "I see you do know. How would you like to come on the show?"

36

Traci felt like she was going to wet her shorts. "On the show?"

"As a guest. I'm sure you've seen Mona's guests?"

"Yes, oh, of course, but how . . . ?"

"Well," Len gave Traci a full-tilt smile, revealing snow-white teeth, "I noticed you're wearing a wedding ring. May I ask how old you are, ma'am? My guess would be about twenty-seven."

Traci blushed furiously, a shade of red so deep it matched her hair. "I'm eighteen."

"Really?" Len was surprised.

"But lots of people say I act much older than I am, like Herb." "Herb?"

"He's my husband. We just got married in the summer."

"And Herb is your age? Quite a young marriage, eh?"

"No, Herb is forty-two."

Len stood there looking at her for a long time. Traci thought something was wrong with him. "Are you okay?"

"Okay?" Len whispered. "Are you kidding? I'm great. This is perfect. God, Mona will love this."

"What?"

"What?" Len snapped out of his thoughts. "What I was about to say is that Mona will be doing a theme on exactly this, older/younger marriages, and we'd love for you to be on the show."

Traci fainted.

★   ★   ★

"He said what?" Traci's father asked later, after Traci had come back to life and found herself on Chester's sofa.

"Me and Herb, we're going to be on Mona."

Chester stared at his daughter. It was a look that Traci knew. It meant disapproval.

"Why?" Chester asked.

"Mona's doing a show on marriages like ours."

37

"Like what?"

"You know, older/younger couples."

Traci watched her father's eyes roll so high in his head that for a brief second she thought they had rolled right out of his head.

"Unbelievable," he said. "Go ahead, make a fool of yourself."

Again, this was a reaction Traci was used to, so she did what she always did. She left, with Chester hollering at her back. "You'll see! You think you're so good. Herb's just using you!"

None of that made any sense to Traci. She didn't have any money, so how could Herb be using her? She loved him and he loved her and that was that, say good-night, pass go and take your two hundred. It was all plain and simple, and now, with Mona Day's show, Traci would be able to tell everyone.

She had to fill out a long form first. Len said it was so Mona would know something about them in advance of the show. This way, when the cameras started rolling, everything would go smooth as silk. She did her best on the forms, but kept getting sidetracked by the television.

The questions weren't hard, but they required long answers.

"When and how did you and your spouse meet?"

I went to Cleardale High in the heights. One day, late in my senior year, Herb needed to come to school to fix one of the bathrooms. Somebody flushed a whole roll of toliet paper down and everything backed up. Herb, my husband-to-be, is a plumber so he was at the school. He came out of the bathroom and ran right into me. His first words were, Excuse me. Later, after school, there he was with his plumbing truck waiting for me. He asked if I wanted to go to a Penguins game so I said sure. That's how we met.

"What attracted you to your spouse?"

He was really cute. He doesn't have a lot of hair, but I think that makes him cuter. He has wide shoulders and brown eyes and very nice teeth. *He's very gentle, even though he looks like he means business. Right from the start he treated me like a woman.*

"How have your family and friends reacted to your marriage?"

They have been awful. My family practically disowned me and it's torture to let Herb near anyone like my father, who is the worst. Most of my old friends are just jealous I think. I say old friends because they hardly don't talk to me anymore. Jenni is going to Penn I think. I mean what's their gripe? Cause I'm happy and they're not?

"Where do you see yourself twenty years from now?"

I'd like to have children of course. I think I'd be a good mother and Herb is willing. He didn't have any kids from his first marriage and it makes him sad sometimes and I don't want him to be sad. He has a great job that he loves. He owns his own plumbing company. We have an apartment now, but are saving for a house. I've been thinking maybe of doing some craftwork, like needlepoint. It would be fun to try and sell some things at the flea market. Herb has encouraged me to do that.

"Is your spouse the first person you had sex with? How is your sex life with your spouse?æ

Herb is the first man I've had sex with. I mean I let Jimmy Gratton feel me up at the junior prom, but I thought he was gonna puke cause I think he was drunk. Sex with Herb is wow! Sometimes I feel like I'm on a cloud. It's like one of those movies on TV late at night, those foreign movies where the woman meets an incredible lover. Well, I met one.

Herb had a slightly different set of questions, Len explained, and Mona would prefer if they didn't share their answers just yet.

"It makes for better television," Len said. "You understand, don't you, Traci?"

She did and she kept to her side of the bargain, but one night in bed Herb told her some of his questions. They weren't all that different from Traci's except the ones about Herb's first wife and something about being a father figure that neither Herb nor Traci understood.

After the questions were all filled out (as well as release papers and proof of identity and copies of their marriage certificate) both of them had to meet with Len again to confirm things and get times and such. It seemed to Traci that Herb and Len didn't get along very well. She figured Herb was about ten years older than Len, but Len kept talking to him like Herb was a boy, like he didn't understand. Herb got steamed, Traci could tell, every time Len asked, "Are you with me?" Traci just squeezed Herb's knee under the table and that pretty much settled things.

On the way home, Herb explained that he ran up against those types all the time.

"What do you mean?" Traci asked.

"I'll go into a house, a real fancy one, out in Oakland someplace. These people don't know squat about pipes, about how their very own three-million-dollar home works. And they give me attitude, you know, like I'm lower than them."

"You ain't, Herb, you're higher than anybody."

"Not to people like that Len guy. He's just another suit, that's all."

Herb called anybody who made more money than him a suit.

"Well, it's not Len we'll be talking to, it's Mona."

Herb smiled. "I know, baby, I know. This is special to you so it's special to me."

Traci beamed.

* * *

There had been a time, in fact only a year earlier, when Traci had had a crush on Chris Bronski, the star running back of the Cleardale Cougars. Actually, he might have been the tight end, but Traci was never able to figure that out. Anyway, sometimes she'd come home after school and just sit and cry in her room and think of Chris Bronski. If anybody had asked, she'd have told them how physical her hurt was, how much her chest ached every time he passed her in the hall. Of course, nobody asked.

This crush—Traci called it love back then—was everything in the world to her. For a while, her life revolved around it. She'd develop elaborate fantasies involving Chris Bronski— them going to the prom, for example. Nothing else could have been as important.

Now, however, when Traci was in Herb's arms, she understood how far she'd traveled in such a short time. She felt so . . . grown up. Herb made her feel this. Just a few weeks ago, in fact, she'd heard that Chris Bronski had been arrested for stealing a car. She wasn't surprised or sad or angry. She just shook her head because he was still so young and Traci wished he had the chance to grow up like she had.

* * *

Her mother called Traci a slut. She laughed at Traci and said that Traci was going to end up face-down in a bottle or a ditch. Gladis had been calling Traci a variety of names for about five years now, ever since the judge had asked Traci to choose between her father and her mother. Traci picked her father, not really because she loved him more but because he was a drunk and Traci felt he couldn't take care of himself.

"And besides," Gladis reminded Traci over the phone, "I don't suppose you've lost any weight since I saw you last, have you?"

"Weight?"

"You know, the stuff between your eyes and your feet. And I heard the television makes you look ten pounds heavier."

Despite this, Mona Day was the one thing Traci and Gladis

had in common, so Gladis agreed to be in the audience for the show. Traci understood her mother would be there only because her mother watched the Mona show even more religiously than Traci did, but Traci thought it might be a good chance, perhaps, to heal some past wounds.

Traci was a healer. It was a title she picked for herself and she carried it like a cross. Her family was a mess, always had been. Just another dysfunctional family in the great primordial dysfunctional family soup. Her older brother died when Traci was two. He drowned at a hockey practice—just crashed through the ice and slipped out of Traci's life along with the current of the mighty Allegheny River. They never found his body, and sometimes Traci imagined her brother's ghostly form, still out there, skating. As near as she could tell, all her uncles and aunts were either drunks, criminals or perverts, so Traci never exactly had a role model around the house.

When Herb stumbled onto the scene, he seemed like the perfect knight. The shining armor was navy blue overalls and the sword was a plunger, but after eighteen years of abuses, Traci wasn't complaining. Herb had a steady job, something her father had never held. Herb was close to his family, and Traci felt wanted by someone, finally. Now she was the matron of her family, the responsible one. She was going to take care of them all and the Mona Day show was going to be like Traci's coming-out party. The new Traci would emerge. The Traci that was a woman.

* * *

The drive to the studio was unbearable.

"You're squirming like an octopus," Herb said, and he laughed.

Herb looked good today, Traci thought. He looked like a businessman in his dark red tie and black suit. Even his nearly bald head shined almost elegantly. Len had made it clear that there was no dress code, but Traci had insisted they wear good clothes. Traci had decided on a nice two-piece outfit, abandoning a dress for blue slacks and a matching coat. She wore on her lapel an ancient brooch, given to her by her grandma Nelli years and years ago. They made a fine couple, like they were important, maybe even going to dinner at a fine restaurant.

The television studio was a massive airplane-hangar-like place with pipes and scaffolding and all sorts of wires and God knew what else. Traci watched the Mona Day show nearly every day, but the studio looked very different in person. Len met them as they made their way toward the stage. The audience wasn't assembled yet and technicians were running this way and that. It was like an ant colony, all those people with wires sticking out of their ears moving like they had important places to go. Even Len looked frazzled. Herb grunted when he saw Len in jeans and a sweatshirt.

"Herb, Traci! You two look fabulous! And so early!"

Len vigorously pumped Herb's hand. "The make-up people aren't here yet, so just relax for a few minutes. Look around if you like, but don't get tangled in any wires."

He flashed them a giant smile, winked and disappeared. Herb and Traci walked around a bit, but finally having no place else to go, they settled into a row of seats near the front of the stage.

"I can't believe we're doing this," Traci whispered.

Herb nodded. "It does seem funny. I mean to be on the other side of the television, you know?"

"It's like we're the stars," Traci said.

Herb smiled. "Stars for the day. Everyone will be interested in us."

Traci poked him in the ribs. "Just us!"

★ ★ ★

The other guests started showing up after a while. There was a couple from Wheeling. The man looked to be in his fifties and was tall, thin and pale. His name was Tommy. His wife, Georgette, outweighed Traci by at least fifty pounds and she physically pulled Tommy around by the ear when she wanted him to move in a certain direction. Traci learned that Georgette was nineteen. The other couple were two bikers from Johnstown, Hank and Denise. They both wore leather from head to foot and Denise was so round, Traci thought of a giant, black beach ball. Hank had tattoos all over his arms and neck. One, a green and black snake, slithered around his chin and disappeared into his leather vest.

Len led all six of them to the back room, a place called the "green" room—called this, Traci found out, because the floor was covered with a rich, green astroturf rug like you'd find at a miniature golf course. In the green room, Len explained to them that most of the show was going to be spontaneous, that Mona had read all their surveys so she knew what to ask and that the audience would ask them questions at various times throughout the show.

"All Mona wants," Len said straightening his tie, "is that you all be honest. Everyone will be interested in your stories and there's nothing to be embarrassed about. You may get asked some hard questions, so keep your chins up and answer as best you can. I'll be back in five."

He left them all sitting there, looking at each other.

"Well, uh, nice to meet you all," Traci said pleasantly.

Everyone nodded. Hank grinned. Georgette picked something from under one of her orange fingernails.

Traci turned to Herb and he only shrugged.

"Do you think mother is here yet?"

Herb shrugged again.

"Is your mother going to be here?" Tommy asked. It was the first thing he'd said all day.

"She said she was," Traci said. "At least I got her a ticket."

44

Tommy nodded. He looked at Georgette, who was still lost in her fingernails, before continuing. "I would have liked for my mom to come."

"Why couldn't she?"

"She'd dead," he said with so little emotion Traci didn't know how to respond.

"Tommy!" Georgette shrieked. "Nobody wants to hear about your dead momma!"

That ended the conversation as Tommy lowered his eyes and went back to staring at the green floor.

Exactly five minutes before the show was to start, Mona walked past the open door to the green room.

"Mona!" Traci leapt up and shouted before she even knew what she had done.

Mona Day, dressed in a smart, dark blue pantsuit and concentrating on reading the sheet of paper on the clipboard in her hand, was the portrait of a successful television personality, from her deep concerned eyes to the startling whiteness of her teeth. From her full, red lips hung a brown cigarette. Traci's shout so startled the host of the Mona Day Show that Mona jumped six inches off the ground, losing the clipboard in the process. A small "poof" of ashes floated up, off her cigarette, and landed squarely in the crease at the beginning of her cleavage. Mona shouted something intangible and clutched frantically at the front of her suit, now spotted with gray and black ash marks. The last Traci saw of Mona Day was the host running for her dressing room, surrounded by stage hands all trying to put out the smoldering fire now growing under Mona's shirt.

* * *

The show started ten minutes late, and Mona was now wearing a light blue dress. Her cheeks looked slightly flushed. Traci had been apologizing to everyone she could, but no one seemed

45

very concerned. Traci even apologized to the other guests, but Hank and Denise just laughed, Georgette clicked her tongue and Tommy stared at his shoes. "It's not a problem, doll," Herb assured her. "We'll be able to speak to Mona later and we'll all have a good laugh."

That's not how it worked out. As Mona warmed up her audience before the cameras started rolling, she would look in Traci's general direction every so often and narrow her eyes. When Mona met her guests finally, she didn't shake Traci's hand.

So, when the familiar theme music for the Mona Day Show started and the audience was clapping and Mona Day was flashing that big smile of hers and walking up the stairs to signal the beginning of her show, Traci was already apprehensive. Traci spotted her mother, but Gladis turned away. The cameras rolled and Traci tried to steel herself.

Mona turned to the camera with the red light and in a loud, concerned voice said, "Women who marry their fathers and men who love overweight women! Today on the Mona Day Show!"

For the second time in a week, Traci fainted dead away.

* * *

Later, much later, Herb and Traci sat at home. Traci hadn't said a word since they had left the studio. They had begged her to pull herself together and go on. Mona herself had knelt beside Traci and with those warm caring eyes Traci knew so well from television, Mona had pleaded with Traci.

"The show must go on, kid," Mona had said. Traci couldn't believe Mona had actually used that line. "The audience wants you, Traci," Mona said. "I want you."

Traci looked straight through her.

Finally, after twenty minutes of everyone from the stage hands to the other guests trying to comfort her, Traci looked up at Herb.

"It's your choice," he said.

"Take me home."

Mona clicked her tongue and stood abruptly. "Oh, fuck it. We're burning studio time. Cut the section and restart the theme. Find me some replacements." Without another word she walked away.

Back at their apartment, Traci sipped from a mug of hot cocoa Herb had made for her. He didn't say anything. He just sat and waited.

"She isn't really a nice person, is she?" Traci asked.

"Who's that, doll?"

"Mona Day."

"No, I guess not."

"I didn't really marry my father, Herb, did I?"

"No."

"And I'm not fat?"

"No."

Traci knew she would be barraged with calls tomorrow from her mother and friends. She knew that tomorrow, like so many other days, she'd have to defend herself. She knew that Chris Bronski was a fantasy, no more real than Santa Claus, and she knew she'd never understand the pipes that rattled under her feet. Also, Traci knew that tomorrow, she'd have to get through her afternoon without Mona Day.

Reptile Dreams

WITH MORE GRACE than a fat man should have, Sam lifted the boa from Sally's trembling hands and wrapped the snake around his own neck and shoulders. "Hold her like a baby," he said.

The snake struggled for a moment before finding Sam's bare, rolling skin an acceptable perch. Sam used a spray bottle to wet the snake. The heat was devastating in the back of the van. Water and sweat rolled off the snake and Sam's 300-pound frame and splashed to the hot floor.

"There, there, Lincoln," Sam cooed, stroking the snake, "Sally don't know you like I do."

Sally crossed her arms and fidgeted. Handling giant pythons wasn't what she expected when the flier advertising for a traveling circus animal trainer appeared on a light pole in Russell Springs. She'd hoped for something less scaly, like goats. Instead, she crossed the Kansas border into Nebraska in the back of a steambath-van handling snakes as part of J. F. Farnsworth's Mobile Minstrels.

"You're doing fine with the others," Sam said. "But you have to stop looking so terrified around Lincoln."

"Lincoln is way bigger than the others," Sally said.

"No difference, just be gentle. Don't forget, Lincoln's our star."

Sam punctuated his statement by scratching the snake's chin, and Sally swore Lincoln looked right at her and smiled.

Sally's stomach churned as Freddy manhandled the controls of the ancient van through the Nebraska plains. Freddy wore only cotton bikini briefs, and tiny pieces of the van's plastic seat had boiled to his back, making it look like he had measles. The circus billed Freddy as "The Incredible Toothpick Boy." Freddy's classic Indian Rubber Man act shocked and disgusted audiences. The highlight of the act happened when Freddy clutched his hands behind his back and pulled them effortlessly over his head. Sally had once made the mistake of asking how the act worked but nearly fainted when Freddy started talking about popping bones out of their sockets.

The van suddenly screeched to a halt. "Red Cloud, Nebraska," Freddy shouted gleefully. He eased his seven-foot frame out of the van and stretched, eliciting a burst of cracks and pops from his abused joints. "Population 856! Plenty of marks at this new jump!"

Sally crawled out from the back of the van into the slightly cooler evening air. "What the hell you jabbering, Freddy?"

Freddy pointed a bony finger at her. "You ain't a newbie no more. Learn the talk."

"Ugh," Sally said and jumped off the hot pavement. "Even the grass is hot."

All around them, the circus was already unfolding. The Mobile Minstrel's twelve trucks were parked on a grassy embankment alongside the road. Horace, the fire eater, and Leon, the magician, were directing a group of a dozen roustabouts in unfolding the big top. She could see the hot and battered desert town, Red Cloud, a mile or so down the road. Through the rising waves of heat, Red Cloud looked blurred, an illusion.

Two children, clad only in overalls, stood by the road and

watched. The boy picked his nose. The girl skipped around him, her pigtails flopping on her shoulders like a wet, dirty mop.

"Look at 'em," Sam spat. "Same thing in every godforsaken town. A goldmine! Come on Sally, lets put ourselves together so these dirt farmers can be entertained for once in their lives."

Mr. Farnsworth didn't allow the Reptile Review near any food stands, so, as usual, Sally and Sam ended up in the far corner of the midway. They assembled the rickety stage, complete with a trap door. Next, they raised a tarpaulin over their area. Sally had painted the tarp herself, dirty orange and black, to resemble snake scales. Some of the paint had begun to blotch and fade from the heat. They pulled a couple dozen folding wooden chairs from the back of one of the supply trucks and arranged them to face the stage. Finally, Sally dragged out their sign. It stood nearly as tall as her and was painted on the straightest piece of barn wood she had been able to find. It read:

FARNSWORTH'S REPTILE REVIEW
See!—Sam and Sally, friends to all reptiles
See!—Lincoln, the largest snake in the world
YOU WON'T BELIEVE YOUR EYES!
Every hour on the hour

Sally and Sam weren't the main attraction of the circus. That honor was reserved for Markus, the amazing half man/half ape, who earned Mr. Farnsworth the biggest gate. Sally was unable to figure out Markus. He actually had all that hair, growing on his body. Last week, Sally had approached Markus for the first time as the ape man was bumming a joint from JoJo the clown behind the Big Top.

"Can I?" she asked timidly.

Markus held out his arm, which was covered with fine, black hair, all of it nearly five inches long. Sally grabbed a handful and pulled. Markus just puffed away, oblivious.

Still, the Reptile Review never failed to attract the locals, and

Sally and Sam could usually count on a packed house for every show. Despite the fact that Sally was still uncomfortable with Lincoln, she had displayed real talent with the other reptiles. And though she would have preferred furry creatures, there were nights she downright enjoyed herself.

"Hey, Saaaaally!"

Mr. Farnsworth's wife, Ellra, came stomping toward the Reptile Review. Ellra was billed as "The Incredible One-Ton Woman" and it wasn't much of an exaggeration. Ellra towered over Sally by a foot and just one of Ellra's calves was the circumference of Sally's waist. Ellra's bright red hair hung lazily down to the back of her knees and as she walked the hair waved back and forth like a horse's tail. Despite the midday sun, Ellra wore an orange sequined dress.

Sally was amazed that Ellra wasn't sweating. "Howdy, Mrs. Ell," Sally said. Only Sally called her that.

"I'll be needing you tonight," Ellra said. "I am in good nature this evening and I want my hair looking special for tonight's opening."

"Sure thing, Mrs. Ell," Sally said. "I'll be over at quarter of seven."

"I'll put in a good word to Mr. Farnsworth," Ellra said over her shoulder as she left. Sally had never met Mr. Farnsworth. He didn't travel with the circus.

Sam grunted. "Wish the big lady liked me like she likes you."

"Don't be jealous, Sam. Mrs. Ell just don't like skinny men!"

They both roared with laughter.

"How long has it been now, girl?" Mrs. Ell asked.

Sally had to think about the question for a while.

The big woman had a small van to herself. Sally stood behind Mrs. Ell, the woman's long orange hair splayed out in Sally's hands.

"About a year, I guess," Sally said running a thick brush over Mrs. Ell's head.

Mrs. Ell turned to face Sally. "I never had a daughter, Sally. But I've watched you over these months and I am quite impressed. As is Mr. Farnsworth."

Sally blushed.

"No, really, girl. You know that whatever you need, you can see me day or night, right?"

"Yes, ma'am."

Mrs. Ell sighed. "Listen, I know it's your birthday."

Sally was shocked. No one knew that. "How did you—?"

Mrs. Ell waved it off. She wrapped a crisp five-dollar bill into Sally's hand. "Eighteen is a special age, Sally. It deserves a special gift. Now, don't you go tellin' everybody how much I spoil you, ok?"

Sally threw her arms around the woman and cried.

With Mrs. Ell satisfied and the Reptile Revue ready for customers, Sally ditched the Minstrels and used the remaining half hour to stroll through town. The money Ms. Ell had given her was going to be put to a good purpose.

She had tied her black hair into a ponytail and pulled on her best pair of boots, the ones her daddy had given her the Christmas before momma died.

She wanted to fit in, but as she walked down Red Cloud's only main street, Sally noticed the people beginning to stare, like they always did in these places. She was an outsider; even worse, a circus freak, despite the fact that in T-shirt and jean shorts Sally looked no different than anyone else on Main Street.

She turned and walked casually into a five and dime, determined to buy a cold bottle of root beer. But there was no ice box here and the store was no different than the other local-yokel food marts sprinkled across the country: a row of canned goods, a row of screwdrivers and a row of toilet paper. Sally closed her eyes and tried to focus on the name the carnies gave to toilet paper. "Honeypot sheets!" she shouted.

She opened her eyes to discover two boys standing in the aisle looking at her.

"Honeypot, what?" the blond one with black jeans and a white T said. He nudged his friend. "You from the carnival?"

Sally nodded.

"You a freak?" the second boy asked. He was fat and red.

"What's wrong with you, you slow or something?" Sally said.

Blondie shrugged. "So what do you do, anyway? Collect tickets?"

"Snakes," Sally said casually.

Blondie looked up, wide-eyed, and the fat boy made a noise that sounded like a broken whistle. "Hear that, Jack?" fat boy giggled. "Snakes, she plays with snakes, pets them and stuff I'll bet, huh."

"Shut up, Frank," Jack said.

"Like little puppy dogs, huh, lady?" Frank said to Jack, but was looking at Sally. "No harm at all for you, huh?"

"Shut up, Frank!" This time, Jack gave Frank a shove that meant business.

Sally could smell their money like she could smell the grass stains on their boots. She addressed Jack. "I suppose you're afraid of snakes, boy."

"I ain't afraid of a few snakes," he said and straightened his shoulders. "I'll be there."

Sally noticed how wide Jack's shoulders were as she opened her soda and took a long, slow gulp. "Yeah, well, one of those snakes is over eight feet long and just last week it swallowed a German Shepherd."

As she left the store, she heard Frank and Jack arguing about where they would find the money to go to the carnival.

She enjoyed the anticipation just before the grounds opened.

By six, a crowd had gathered at the entrance to the midway. The carnival was veiled in quiet as the various performers and workers made last-minute preparations. Sally sat at the foot of her snake-show stage and waited. Her first show was at seven and she would spend the next hour rounding up an audience. She had changed into her show costume: high black boots and a purple oversized skirt with a variety of scarves and tassels. She let her black, straight hair grow out, and it already touched the small of her back. Sally modeled her look on pictures of gypsies she found at libraries along the way.

She sighed. As always, she felt foolish. Plus, the tassels got in the way of the snakes. The costume was personally approved of by Mr. Farnsworth, however, or at least Mrs. Ell told Sally so.

She thought of her father and how he would react to her appearance. It made her grimace. Sally's daddy, Rev. Harum Webster, spread the Word in Russell Springs and preached like the town was filled with demons and deceivers. Sally remembered standing in a crowd, listening to her father's street corner lecturing and feeling the crowd's hate and amusement, and worst of all, the pity leveled toward her own father.

He hated her decision to join the carnival. After mother died, father wanted to branch out, to preach across the state.

"Sally," he had told her, "the carnival is filled with misfits and the damned. I need your help elsewhere, in places larger than Russell Springs. The place for you is with family."

The real reason her father wanted to leave was that the Town Council had voted to ban street corner solicitation. The fact that Harum Webster's name was specifically mentioned in the ordinance required a level of humility that no teenager was capable of mustering.

"You're crazy," she had told him as he packed his things. "If you think I'm gonna follow around a Bible-thumpin' loon into every desert and back-woods hick town—"

He slapped her, hard enough to split her lip and leave a

week-long bruise. "You'll follow, child. Momma would have wanted that."

She had followed all right, and all the way to the train station Sally had turned over in her head those last words he had spoken to her. Momma wouldn't have wanted that. Momma had always spoken about how wonderful life was in big places, in big cities with museums and fancy restaurants. Momma would never have allowed Harum to strike his daughter, or anyone for that matter. So, when they arrived at the train station, Sally told her father she wasn't going. The train began to pull away and Harum had to make a choice.

"You can't leave family, Sally," he told her. "You will never be able to leave."

He then climbed onto the train, and Sally stood and watched his wide back sink into a seat and out of sight.

"Honey." It was Sam. "Sally, snap out of it, girl, we have a show to run!"

Sally blinked as though she had just awakened from a dream and smiled. "I know, Sam, I know."

The first part of the Reptile Review was easy, just some simple handling while Sam lied and exaggerated about how dangerous the snakes were. Most of the reptiles were of an extremely harmless variety, barely more than garden snakes. The circus workers collected snakes as they passed through towns. Sometimes customers would bring snakes that had become too big to care for and the circus would take them. Other times, Sam would go on snake collecting excursions, visiting farms to collect exotic-looking reptiles.

There were some venomous snakes at the review, but Sam kept those in a special crate only for display. Sam even had a rattlesnake named Petey, long since defanged, but its ancient rattle gave Sally many nightmares.

Sally had even touched up some of Sam's snakes to make

them appear more exotic. Sally studied pictures in snake books as they traveled, so she could paint garden snakes to resemble coral snakes or other colorful varieties.

In the audience that the Snake Review attracted, no one ever knew the difference. In every show, Sam made up newer and better names.

"And now, my brave audience," Sam would say, swaggering back and forth across the stage, his great weight causing the timbers to groan and squeak, "behold the deadly Nigerian Prairie Cobra. Note the puffy orange venom sacs. This creature, once thought extinct, suddenly resurfaced several years ago when scientists realized the snake performed an ancient ritual known as the hibernation trance. The snake drops into a deep hibernation period once every century and stays asleep for fifteen years!"

He would speak with such authority and with such flair and total commitment to every word that the audience had no choice but to believe. Sam's eyes stared down disbelievers. The audience was mostly kids and teenagers, and most of them were boys. Sally thought she saw the boys from the five and dime and her fears were confirmed a moment later when Jack stood up and shouted. "That ain't no cobra! I seen pictures of cobras and they got thick heads and are a lot bigger!"

Sally smiled and glanced at Sam, who shrugged and stood aside. The boy had it right, of course—the snake in question was a harmless garter snake that Sally had painted. It never occurred to her to question why Jack might know the difference between a garden snake and a cobra. She just stepped down off her stage, the snake in tow, and grinned as the crowd in the first row gasped and leaned back away from her as far as their seats would let them. She tickled and prodded the snake to squirm and then acted as though she was having trouble holding it.

"Would you like to see for yourself, young man?" she asked while moving toward him.

Frank sat next to Jack and tugged on his sleeve.

"Come on, Jack, this ain't funny," Frank pleaded. "That's a real snake, she's coming over here."

"Here, I insist you have a closer look," Sally continued, relentlessly moving toward Jack. "This way you can see for yourself how dangerous this snake is."

The young man took two steps back with every one Sally took toward him. A thin string of sweat broke out on his forehead, and his neck and shoulders became tense. Finally, as he reached the tent flap exit, Sally pushed the snake toward him and with a feeble yelp the boy stepped out and was lost in the twilight. Frank was frozen in his seat, his face white. Sally turned to the crowd and shrugged. "Any more doubters?"

She was rewarded with applause.

The carnival crowd had wandered away, leaving behind a trail of stale popcorn and trampled grass. Sally rested her head on the grass and felt the cool midnight dew slide down her neck. The carnival had just closed another money-making weekend. Tomorrow they would leave Red Cloud, and Sally didn't mind one bit. She was restless. The carnival's freedom had begun to feel like an illusion. Sally considered dropping out of the circus as they passed through the next big city like Hastings or maybe Omaha and maybe finding steady work, at a pet shop or a zoo.

Sally thought about her dad as she watched the universe spiral in the mirror-like surface of a small pond. She tried to imagine a place like New York City, but couldn't. All those people, all those lives—she'd been warned countless times about the evils of places like that. Father and even `Farnsworths warned her of many things.

A branch snapped behind Sally. She heard breathing, and scrambled to her feet.

Jack stood behind her, next to a tall oak tree. He offered her a half-empty bottle.

"What do you want?" Sally asked.

"I followed you here," Jack said. "I followed you all the way from your trailer."

Sally figured the distance back to the circus area to be about 300 yards: too long to run and too far away for anyone to hear if she yelled. She took a quick look around. An apple-sized rock lay at her feet. The boy darted toward her and Sally dropped to the ground, grabbed the rock and slammed it as hard as she could into his ankle.

Jack drooped like a deflated tire.

"Aw Christ," he whined. "Why'd you do that, that's gonna bruise."

He had dropped the bottle, which Sally now noticed was a root beer, and was rubbing his ankle furiously. Sally stood there, looking from the rock in her hand to the root beer to the boy.

"Shit," he said again. The skin was broken and a deep red welt was beginning to form around the cut.

"What the hell is wrong with you?" she sputtered. "What's the big idea sneaking up on a girl at midnight?"

"A root beer," he moaned. "I just wanted to bring you a root beer."

Jack plopped down next to her and rubbed his ankle.

"Sorry," Sally said. "You really were just bringing me a root beer?"

He nodded and pushed a thick strand of blond hair out of his eyes. Sally noticed that his arms seemed too long for his body and his skin was dark and rough like he had spent his whole life in the sun. She shook her head.

"Sorry," she said.

"I want to join your carnival," Jack said.

"What?"

"The carnival, I want in."

Sally jumped up and turned her back to him. "I don't have that kind of—"

"I have to get out of here," he said. "My father will kill me sooner or later. Or I'll kill him. Either way, I have to leave."

Sally listened with her back toward him.

"I never do enough, he says. Never. We fought yesterday. I gave him a black eye and he told me that next time he saw me he was gonna beat me to death. He said that. My own father." Jack shook his head and took a deep breath. "I—I can juggle or put up stuff. I really liked your act, really. I'm sorry for yelling out like that. I just wanted you to notice me."

Sally turned. "You can juggle?"

"Well, sure. Look, I pack freight at the five and dime. Sometimes I even unload the pickup on my own." Then, almost under his breath, he said. "I could even help you with your act, you know, if you need help."

She sighed. "I'll talk to Mr. Farnsworth's wife tomorrow. Maybe we could use another driver or an extra hand for the setups."

"Okay, whatever," Jack said. "You'll see how hard I can work. Like ten men."

"Be there at 6:00 a.m.," she laughed.

"You got it!" Jack bounded forward, but stopped short of hugging Sally. Instead, he clumsily shook her hand before turning and limping back into the woods.

"You're going to work, Jack!" Sally shouted.

Jack turned toward her, and even in the moonlight, Sally could see his face before he turned into the shadows. His smile made her think of bigger dreams than reptiles.

By the time the carnival reached South Dakota, Jack had been with them for two weeks and already Sally could see a change. She sat lazily by her trailer and watched Jack help strike the big top.

His blond hair was pressed against his forehead in a tangle of sweaty knots. Streaks of golden perspiration lined his shirtless chest and back. For the hundredth time that week, Sally wondered if he really was only sixteen and if that really mattered.

The day before, Sally had brought Jack over to the Reptile Review truck and introduced him to some of the snakes. Jack seemed to have a real affinity for Lincoln. Plus, Jack didn't seem to mind Lincoln's weight.

Jack wanted to know if Lincoln ever bit her.

"Lincoln? Gosh, no," Sally had said. "Lincoln is harmless as a puppy. Even the snakes that do bite are harmless, garden snakes, that type of thing. The dangerous ones are just kept in crates for show."

"He was a good choice," Sam said, coming up to Sally. "Best newbie we've ever had."

"Hey!' Sally said.

"Except for you, kid, except for you."

"That's better, Sam."

"You like him," Sam said.

"You're so sure, huh?"

Sam just smiled. "I've been thinking about what you asked earlier. I think maybe we could use Jack in the reptile show."

"Really? When?"

"Talk to him now. We can use him tonight."

Sally hopped off the stage and trotted toward Jack. Over her shoulder, she called, "Thanks Sam!"

Jack was waiting for her.

"Wanna take a break?" she asked.

Together, they walked off to the side of the circus grounds. He was breathing hard and Sally had to fight back the urge to trace her finger along his sweat-coated chest.

"Guess what?" she said. "How'd you like to work the reptiles?"

Jack's eyes got wide. "With you?"

"I talked to Sam. He said okay. And I want you."

Jack grinned.

This time, they did hug and it was a while before they parted.

That evening, Jack and Sally sat together off stage waiting for the show to begin. Jack had gone through wardrobe and had picked out another brightly colored genie outfit—to match Sally's, he told her.

Tonight would be easy. Jack would help move some props, and help Sally and Sam move the reptiles back and forth among the cages. Sally sat next to Jack, silent. She didn't even look at him. Only their hands touched, his resting on hers. The crowds came in, the lights glared; there was laughing and cotton candy and the sounds of a carnival on a Saturday night drowning out the hiss of snakes.

The heat didn't let up that evening and only a couple dozen people were in the audience when Sam began his introductions.

Sally went over some last-minute instructions with Jack. About twenty-five snakes were used over the course of one show, and Jack had been given a crash course earlier in the day on how to identify each of them. Each crate was numbered, so when Sally would need a certain snake, the plan was simply to step slightly off stage and call for a number. Jack would take the snake Sally needed and they would switch. Occasionally some props would be needed, and Jack would come up on stage with Sam and Sally for the grand finale, which would involve stretching Lincoln out to full length.

When they had practiced earlier, Jack had flown from crate to crate like he had done it a thousand times before. He handled the snakes with a delicacy that surprised Sally, almost holding them at his fingertips.

"You nervous?" Sally asked Jack.

He shook his head.

"You look cute," she said.

"Will this make you happy?"

"What?" Sally asked.

"Working with me. Me being here."

Sally tilted her head to meet his eyes. "Yes. Yes, I like being with you, wherever we are."

"I'm doing this for you," Jack whispered.

But before Sally could question Jack, Sam announced her name. She kissed Jack, and left for the stage.

The show was difficult that night. The heat made Sally uncomfortable, and the snakes seemed confused and hard to handle. She nearly dropped one, its skin suddenly feeling wet and clammy. Jack raced between crates, wiping his brow. The snake area was a jumble of crates and thick bags, and Jack had moved some of the crates around to make it easier to bring out the next snake.

Sally didn't have the time or the ability to figure out his system, but it worked for a while. She was impressed with his organization. She would turn to return a snake and the snake's tank would always be waiting for her, number side out, while Jack fished out the next specimen.

Halfway through the show, as Sally finally began to find her rhythm and as the small crowd began to respond, she turned toward Jack in time to see a black and yellow blur shoot out from one of the crates and land squarely in the fleshy webbing between Jack's left thumb and forefinger. Jack stumbled back, knocking over several tables.

"Jack!" Sally moved toward him.

Jack seemed frozen in place as escaped snakes moved around his feet, like waves. He looked up when Sally called, meeting her gaze, not even realizing that the Coral snake that had bitten him was still attached to his hand, writhing, its black head pumping like a heartbeat.

By 2:00 a.m. Sally had been drunk for four hours. The early part of the night had been a blurred nightmare of sobbing and screaming, which finally ended when Sam had physically carried her to bed. The hard whiskey sat like glue in her stomach. Sally's tent was very cold. Everything was cold.

At some point in the evening, Sam had scolded her. "The show must go on, kid," he had said.

"That a stupid thing to say!" she screamed at him. Sam had left Sally to her own misery and that's when she started drinking.

She threw an empty bottle at the tent wall, but it only thudded lightly before falling, unbroken, to the grass. Sally walked over and smashed the bottle, digging her heel into the glass until her foot bled.

"Shit!" she was crying again.

"Don't let the anger tear you apart, Sally," said a voice.

Sally looked up, startled. Mrs. Farnsworth stood at the tent flap. "I'm sorry about what happened tonight," she said.

"I—but—"

"It wasn't your fault," Mrs. Farnsworth said firmly.

"Yes! Yes it was!" Sally blurted. "He must have mixed up the crates! He didn't know. We started him too fast!"

In two long strides, Mrs. Farnsworth had crossed the distance between them and slapped Sally. The woman's meaty hand sounded like the snapping of a wet washcloth across Sally's cheek. "It was no one's fault. No one knew and nothing could be done in time! Do you hear me, Sally?"

Sally nodded, feeling the sting of the slap, tears streaming down her cheeks, lost.

"Good. Did you destroy the snake?" Mrs. Farnsworth asked.

Sally nodded mechanically. "Sam did."

"Excellent," Mrs. Farnsworth said quietly. "The customers who were there were none the wiser of what happened. We leave tomorrow and people will forget this ever happened. You'll let me take care of this, won't you, Sally?"

"Yes."

"I have a friend in Kansas who will help me. You'll see, this will work to our advantage. You're a good girl, Sally. You're part of our family and I'll take care of you." Mrs. Farnsworth was gone, the sound of her heavy footsteps fading like Sally's tears. Sally took several deep breaths and threw herself onto her cot. Even by squeezing her eyelids, she could find no sleep.

After being bitten, Jack had stumbled away from the stage and fallen into Sally's arms. The image of Jack's shocked expression and Sam's desperate attempts to revive him all seemed unreal to Sally. Jack's skin became pale and sweaty and within minutes, as stage hands ran to find a doctor, Jack's throat had swelled and Sam couldn't get any air past Jack's bloated tongue. In the fading light of the tent, as a disappointed crowd was herded out into the night, Jack's skin turned blue and he shuddered once before dying. His eyes remained open, and focused— in death—on Sally.

A few weeks later, the circus had rumbled into another small town in the middle of Montana. It was Saturday evening and two tiny freckle-faced girls stood staring at the circus's newest attraction.

"Touch it, Jeannie," the golden-haired one prodded her shy friend.

Jeannie reached a tiny hand toward the glass coffin, but was stopped by the attendant.

"Ah, ah, girls," a brightly dressed gypsy girl scolded them, "this is a very valuable discovery. We shouldn't tamper."

"Is he really real?" Jeannie asked.

"You bet he's real," the gypsy said. "We found him in the Yukon. We call him Icicle Jack because he was frozen and preserved. He's over one thousand years old!"

"Wow!" both girls gasped at once.

"Now run along," said the gypsy.

The girls stared a moment longer at Icicle Jack's cold, white body and thick yellow hair. His open mouth was frozen in a silent scream and the girls mimicked this pose before skipping off, giggling to themselves.

Sally watched them go, her face a blank, impassive mask. She thought of her family as she ran a trembling hand across the frigid glass tomb.

More Than Breath

CHARLIE'S ATTENTION was focused on the young saxophonist. The musician's jacket was damp with sweat and he was playing as hard as he could blow, his cheeks puffed and red. Charlie covered his face with his own perspiring hands and inhaled deeply. Sweat was one thing Charlie knew.

It was July and Charlie marked this time of year with free jazz concerts at the waterfront. To the left of the stage, the light from the Ben Franklin Bridge danced in the still water of the Delaware River as a feeble breeze failed to pierce the suffocating heat. From behind him, the cheers and hoots and whistles of a thousand jazz fans floated past his ears, unheard. Right now, all that mattered was the saxophone player.

Charlie could picture—no, feel—the scene from all those years ago. The bar was called the Tin Can and back then it was *the* bar for jazz in Philadelphia.

`The owner's name had been Cat Cutter and he couldn't play a note himself. In fact, Cat told everyone who would listen that he was tone deaf. Charlie recalled the evening Cat had called him aside and spoken to him in whispered tones.

"How long you been playin' here, Chaz?"

"'Bout three years, Cat. Every Thursday for three years." Charlie said this with pride. He knew there was a long list of jazzmen who'd sell their sisters for the chance to be a regular at the Tin Can.

"Chaz, how you been lately? I mean, you've been sounding good, but, you know . . . is your head together?"

"Yeah, Cat, I'm together. I don't do that shit for gigs, man. You know that."

"Yeah, Yeah, I hear you."

Cat was a little man, barely five feet, but he was built thick. As long as Charlie had known him, Cat's eyes had remained unreadable. They were unreadable now.

"Listen, Chaz," Cat said, putting his arm around Charlie's waist. Cat was clearly uneasy. His voice grew so soft that Charlie had to strain to hear. "Next week, there's someone coming— someone I want to impress."

"What, a client?"

"No, a musician. I think he might want to play a little. He'll need a horn, though."

"What, you want me to back him?"

Cat nodded.

"Sure, who is he?"

"Piano player. You'll do this for me, won't you, Chaz?"

"Yeah. Who is he?"

Cat pulled a long cigar out of his coat and lit it. "This is supposed to be a surprise visit. So don't let anyone know about this."

"Cat, who is it?"

"Promise me you won't let anyone know."

"I swear on my grandmother's grave." Charlie was laughing now. "Who am I playing with next week?"

"Thanks, Chaz, I know you won't let me down."

"Cat, wait—" It was too late. Cat had disappeared into the smoke and sound. Charlie was left standing at the bar. "Hey, Frankie, give me a gin and tonic." The bartender slid the drink to him and he put the cool glass to his dry lips.

It came back empty. He tipped the bottle up into the light

from the stage, just to be sure. Nothing. Behind him, the steady rustle of the crowd sounded far away, like leaves in the wind. He knew there were hundreds, thousands, of people elbow to elbow on the concrete bleachers, but Charlie was alone in the small half-circle in front of the stage. He was alone because no one would come near him, but it didn't matter.

"Get out of the way, you bum!" someone shouted behind him.

Charlie didn't hear. He stutter-stepped right up to the stage until he was standing directly under the sax player. The band was Max Roach's quartet. Charlie reached back into his memory, trying to remember if he'd ever played with Max Roach. Unlikely.

The sax player missed a note and the sound was flat and thin. Charlie figured the crowd didn't even hear it, didn't even realize a beat was missed. Charlie knew. He knew how it felt to miss, like a lost heartbeat.

"You're missing it," his father was saying, "Put your weight behind it, all your weight. Move into a note like you'd move into a fastball."

Charlie let the heavy saxophone drop between his knees. Practice was nearly over and he was winded. "This isn't sports. I ain't trying to hit a home run. All I need to hit a note is my breath."

Eli Webster shook his head. "Music's more than breath, it's body. Every bone and drop of blood has to play every note."

"Fastballs? Blood? I don't even know what you're talkin' about!"

Charlie's father smiled, shaking his head. His sixteen-year-old son looked at him with a long face and wide eyes. Eli Webster was a patient man, a man who knew when to fight and when to concede. He knew the difference between Charlie's mock refusals and when the boy was really tired and had had enough. Since Charlie's mother had left five years ago, Eli had had the opportunity to spend a lot of time with his son. Music was one thing they had in common, perhaps the only thing. He knew pushing the boy would only make an already difficult life even worse.

"What are you in such a hurry for anyway?" Eli asked.

"Nothin'. Just meeting some of the guys at the court."

"Alright, Charlie, we'll pick up tomorrow."

Without a word, the boy bolted toward the door.

And knocked.

"Yeah?" Cat's voice was raspy and low. "Come on in, Chaz."

It was the day before Thursday and for the first time since Charlie had worked at the Tin Can, he was nervous. Cat had all but ignored Charlie's questions.

"Take a seat."

Cat's office was small and sparse. His chair, however, was a gigantic leather throne in which Cat seemed to enclose himself. Today, Charlie's boss was wearing a light brown cardigan and tan turtleneck. It seemed to Charlie as if the chair itself was talking.

"You're all set, right, Chaz?"

Charlie nodded. He had just come from the bar and the room was spinning slightly; not much, but Charlie thought it better if he didn't do much talking.

"Tomorrow's an important night for me . . . and for you."

Charlie just kept nodding.

"Everything all right at home? I mean with the old lady."

More nodding, except everything wasn't all right. Charlie and Zora had fought again that morning. It was getting worse each time. This time, however, Charlie had hit her. Not hard and he regretted it instantly, but the deed was done.

Zora had been difficult lately, forcing Charlie to practice when she wasn't home. Or, sometimes, he'd come to the Tin

69

Can, after closing, and practice there on the cold, empty stage in front of the upturned chairs. Of course, practices at the Tin Can were growing shorter and shorter as one of the bartenders or janitors would always hand Charlie a flask.

"I'll be fine, Cat," he managed to say without slurring.

But everything was not fine.

He just couldn't figure out the problem as the screams and curses of his parents carried like echoes all the way down four flights of stairs and out onto the street. Little Charlie Webster stood there on the hot, dry sidewalk looking up at his apartment building. Embarrassed.

"Hey, man, is that your folks?" The question came from Jackie Burns, Charlie's closest friend; at least as close a friend as a kid can have in fourth grade.

"Yeah, it's them."

This wasn't new. Jackie had asked that question a dozen times in the last month alone. Charlie wondered why he even asked anymore. Maybe Jackie was just trying to be polite.

"What are you going to do?" Jackie asked.

Good question. If Charlie walked in, in the middle of a fight, his angry father might turn on him. Then again, if he didn't go in, he'd miss practice. Clearly, Charlie would get a beating if that happened.

"I better go in." An acceptance of an unavoidable fate.

"Okay." Jackie shrugged. "See you later."

"Good-bye."

That was all Zora said. Good-bye. There was no screaming or crying; nothing that would normally be associated with one partner leaving another forever; just good-bye and the closing of a door. Zora left Charlie in 1962, one year after Charlie had failed so miserably at the Tin Can and five months after Charlie had been fired by Cat.

Charlie was drunk for one straight month after that, not even venturing outside his three-room West Philadelphia apartment. He came out of his stupor one evening when the alcohol ran out. He was penniless and without a wife. His clothes had become dirty, sweat-soaked rags and he wondered when (or if) he had changed them since Zora left. With shaking hands and the sound of his heartbeat pounding in his head, Charlie looked out the apartment's only window and realized it was Christmas. Across the street, in the window of a hardware store, a plastic, browning Santa blinked madly in the dull glare of a streetlight. Just blinking . . .

. . . like the orange and yellow spotlights that seemed to swerve madly on the stage. Charlie wished the lights would stop moving and just focus on the saxophone player. Better yet, Charlie wished the lights would shine on the saxophone, the instrument itself. Nothing else mattered but the golden gleam of the saxophone. Nothing else captured Charlie's life, Charlie's past, quite so completely. He hadn't held a musical instrument in nearly ten years, but the cool feel of metal, growing hot with breath and sweat, was a sensation he would never lose.

The band was taking a break now, leaving the stage to happy applause. Charlie was bumped and pushed by several elbows and shoulders as the crowd surged and stretched. Charlie pushed himself up against the stage as close as he could to avoid the glares of the crowd. Someone, a tall man, brushed Charlie's face and Charlie instinctively put his hands to his mouth, to protect his lips from injury.

It was a habit he'd picked up from his father.

"To communicate with music," his father had said to him one afternoon during practice, "you need your lips. Your teeth. Your tongue. Protect the physical part of your art just as you protect the mental part."

Eli Webster had brought his young family to Philadelphia

two months before Charlie was born. Eli had found some minor success in New York. He had also found his wife, Charlie's mother, Camille. Eli and Camille hadn't met in a jazz bar or even a music store. They met waiting in line at a street vendor. One month later Camille was pregnant. She was seventeen and Eli was nineteen.

Philadelphia gave them the benefit of a new start away from Camille's unforgiving family and Eli's guilt. The jazz scene in Philly was strong and the war was still a year away. Charlie was born amid hope and happiness in the Spring of 1941 and Eli Webster was determined to make sure his son had a good life.

It was the good life that Cat was talking about. Charlie tried hard to remain focused, but his head was pounding.

"This is where it's at, Chaz. This is living for the day." It was quarter to midnight. Cat's surprise guest hadn't shown up yet, but the place was jammed anyway. The rumors of a name act showing had started circulating weeks ago. Cat had spent most of the week tuning and polishing the Tin Can's stage piano. "All he needs is keys," he mumbled all week to himself. "Give this man keys and it doesn't have to be a Steinway."

Charlie had just finished a three-hour set. His neck was sore and his lips were puffy and tender. Earlier that day, hours before his first set at the Tin Can, Zora had threatened to leave him. It was the first time she had done that. The argument had started like all the rest. Zora wanted to know when Charlie was going to start taking his life seriously and find a job with a future. Charlie told her if she would only come and see him play for once, she would understand how serious music was to him.

No one ever came to see Charlie play. He had fans, of course, customers he would see every week, their eyes closed, heads nodding to Charlie's music. He loved them, but they were different. Sometimes, he wanted Zora to come and listen so badly that he would feel sick to his stomach. He wished his father were still alive. His father listened.

A commotion at the door turned Charlie's attention away from Cat. A mob of people was huddled around a figure and it was a few moments before Charlie realized who it was. Cat's surprise guest had just walked in and Charlie felt his fingers go numb. Tiny pins and needles began creeping up his hands and the hair on his arms stood up. It was a sensation Charlie had felt only once before, the moment he met Zora.

It was the one and only time that Zora had heard Charlie play. High school didn't interest Charlie, but his father had forced him to go, to stick with it. Charlie was only eighteen when he started playing in bars and clubs. At first, he'd play maybe once a week to drunks and prostitutes at South Philly dives. His father landed Charlie his first few gigs, cashing in on some owed favors that even Charlie never asked about. After a while, though, as Charlie began outplaying the house musicians, it was clear that he wouldn't be playing in dives for long. Zora walked into his life during the first gig that Charlie headlined.

The club was called Julian's. Outside the tiny jazz room, a poster read "Philly's own Chaz Webster and his Trio." There was a glossy black and white photo of Charlie on stage under the words. In the photo, Charlie's eyes were closed. Sweat ran down the contours of his high cheeks. His saxophone glimmered like a star.

The musicians weren't really Charlie's group. They had been provided by Julian's. It didn't matter to Charlie, though. He played that night as if he owned the place, and he did. His father had been in that crowd, and after the show, as the two of them sat at the bar, Eli Webster turned to his son and said, "You're a professional, Charlie. I cried out there in the audience tonight."

"Dad, there were only twenty people out there."

His father nodded. "And they heard you play like you were playing to twenty thousand."

It was much later, after Eli had gone home and Charlie sat alone at the bar, that Zora walked up. She sat at the stool next to Charlie and, without looking at him, said, "You're good."

"Thanks." Charlie turned and knew immediately that he would marry Zora.

She had come to Julian's for dinner with friends, despite not liking jazz, or any music for that matter. Charlie felt this displayed an open mind and a willingness to try new things. Zora gave Charlie a new vibrancy, someone to work hard and practice and become the best for. All this, he knew in the first minutes of their meeting.

It wasn't until Eli's funeral that Charlie began to realize Zora would leave him. Charlie and Zora had been married for seven months when Eli was found dead in his apartment of a heart attack. Eli Webster was only thirty-nine. Camille came to the funeral. It was the first time Camille and Zora met, and the last.

Camille was a wreck and Charlie found his mother's reaction disquieting in light of the fact that she had been the one to leave the family. She had abandoned Eli and Charlie for reasons still not clear to anyone but herself.

"Mother?" Charlie approached her slowly, carefully, as she sat alone on a small couch. Her eyes were wet from crying.

"Charlie." She wrapped her arms around her son and cried. Charlie hadn't seen or heard from her in months, but he held her anyway. It was at that moment that Charlie and his mother nearly attained an understanding of each other.

"You must be Camille," Zora said to the tear-streaked face of Charlie's mother.

Zora wrapped her arm in Charlie's and slowly but forcefully coaxed Charlie and his mother out of their embrace.

"I'm so sorry," Zora said.

Camille stood for a moment looking at Zora.

"This is Zora, momma."

"Zora?" Camille swayed slightly before turning away to the prone body of Eli.

"She's odd," Zora whispered to Charlie.

Charlie said nothing.

Later, before he left, he tried one last time to get through to his mother. Zora was waiting in the car and Charlie pretended he had left his gloves inside. Camille was waiting for him, as though she knew he'd come back.

"Good-bye, Mother."

Charlie's mother took his hand and kissed it gently.

"Why did you leave him?" Charlie asked.

She smiled sadly. "Because I didn't deserve him."

"But—." Outside, Zora was leaning on the horn and Charlie glanced over his shoulder, losing his train of thought. When he turned back, Camille was gone. With a resigned sigh, he pulled up his collar and walked out into the rain, where Zora waited.

It was rain for sure. Tiny, cold raindrops began to sting Charlie's cheeks and neck. It was midway through Max Roach's second set when the clouds moved in and the wind began throwing the river against the shoreline, which was only a few feet behind the stage. Already people were starting to leave and the band was eyeing the suddenly changing weather. Charlie sensed the shift in the crowd and felt a familiar desperation rising in him. He didn't want anyone to leave. From his position at the head of the stage, he had become a part of the band. To abandon the music, even if only to stay dry, was like abandoning a primal and important part of life. The music was the most important thing, he wanted to scream. The sounds. The flow. But he said nothing. Instead, Charlie watched as the band stopped and scrambled off the stage and the people turned their backs and sought the comfort of home.

The rain was pounding Penn's Landing now and Charlie

stood for a moment longer trying to decide where to sleep tonight. Normally, the waterfront and its long benches and many overhangs provided warmth and shelter, but tonight everything was wet and the band's early departure left Charlie feeling empty. He shuffled off to his left and found himself heading toward the band trailers. A heaviness had settled upon him and he thought, perhaps, he could get one more glimpse of the saxophone. It would make him feel better.

"Have a drink, Charlie, you'll feel better."

It was Frankie, the bartender at the Tin Can. Charlie swallowed the alcohol in one long gulp, not even tasting it. It was nearly three in the morning. Cat's guest piano player had gone home and Charlie sat in the club, nearly alone, wondering how he could have been so off.

"Cheer up, Charlie. It wasn't that bad. You sounded fine."

Fine wasn't good enough. Charlie wanted to sound the best. He wanted to be the best. Up until tonight, he had thought perhaps he was the best. Charlie had worked hard, trying to follow the fingers of the Man. The piano player wasn't just good. He was a genius. He played without form, improvising whole numbers. His style was so complicated and precise, Charlie couldn't begin to predict where the notes would fall next. Charlie had spent most of the evening just trying to make up for missed cues.

He had heard stories about the piano player's level of accomplishment. He even owned some of his albums. It hadn't mattered tonight. Charlie had been off, plain and simple. He was lacking and it showed. After the set, the Man had turned to Charlie and smiled warmly. "Good sound," he had said. But by then it was too late. Charlie knew he had failed.

"You were a little off today, huh?" It was Cat. Charlie's boss had slid onto the stool to Charlie's right.

"Yeah."

Cat nodded and stared across the bar at the mirror. He ran his fingers through his curly black hair and wet the ends of his mustache. "Nobody can be on every day," Cat said.

"Yeah."

Cat sighed. "Yeah. Well, I'll catch you next week, Chuck."

Next week Charlie was worse. The week after that and the several that followed, Charlie didn't even remember. Looking back, it was impossible for him to remember when he stopped practicing. Did he sell his saxophone after the divorce or after Cat fired him? The days and years that followed were a blur. His fingers became thick and red and his breath grew short.

By the time Zora left, Charlie's life was over.

He couldn't believe it was all over. It didn't seem fair that the weather should stop music. Charlie felt that music was beyond weather. That, in fact, music was magical and you can't stop magic for any reason. Once it starts, it has to play itself out.

Charlie found himself standing in front of the band trailer, staring at the yellow light coming from inside. The rain was rattling the aluminum siding and nearly drowning out the happy sounds from within. After a long time, as dirty water dripped from his nose, his cheeks and his eyelids, and his ragged shoes had become heavy and cold, the band left the trailer.

The sax player stepped out first. In one hand he held an umbrella. In the other was the sax case. Charlie moved forward and moved toward the case.

"Can I see it, man?" he asked. "I just want to have a look."

The musician saw him coming and stepped back and out of the way. Charlie lost his footing and fell, sprawling across the wet pavement.

By the time Charlie turned, the band was gone. The saxophone was gone. He sat there a while longer, rubbing his now scraped and raw hands before moving to a bench by the water. Against the glare of lights off the river, the storm reminded him of Christmas and the colors were red and yellow. He remembered the blinking Santa and the feel of hot metal against cold fingers. Charlie closed his eyes, pretending he was a little boy again, and slowly, the rain seemed to subside.

Blue Lady

"GREAT WEATHER FOR A DUCK," the lady with the light blue umbrella says to me as we wait for the train.

I nod, step forward and look down the tracks. They are empty. The rain has changed from a slight drizzle to a ripping downpour. It looks like there is no air, only water.

"I said, this is good weather for a duck."

I notice she is wearing light blue button-up booties, plastic, the same shade as her umbrella. She's waiting for me to say something.

"Yes," I mumble, "a duck." I wish the train would come.

We both stand there for a while. The train stop near my home is flimsy, barely more than a plastic bus shelter, and I can hear every drop of water. It pounds the leaves off the trees and slaps loudly against the plastic bag in the garbage can.

I bunch together the collar of my suit coat and make sure my briefcase is staying dry. After six years of standing at this stop, every morning at this time, I don't remember ever seeing her. Out of the corner of my eye I notice the lady is slowly rocking back and forth on her booties. She fumbles for a while in her raincoat and pulls out a soggy and crinkled packet of Chiclets. It looks like she's had it for a while.

"Want one?" she asks.

"No, I'm allergic to Chiclets." I roll my eyes.

"I have an aunt who's allergic to Chiclets," she says somberly.

I nod again. I wonder about her aunt. The lady stuffs the rest of the gum into her mouth. After a few minutes of vigorous chewing, she starts to hum the theme from *The Love Boat*.

I sigh and push my hands deep into my pockets, hoping I can find room in there for the rest of my body. The train is now five minutes late. Water drips from the tip of my nose to my lips. I pretend I'm Socrates and have just swallowed the fatal hemlock.

"I was an extra in *Rocky V*," she suddenly says. "I was a bus rider."

"It will look good on your resume."

She turns her umbrella to the left, and I am finally able to get a good look at her. I notice that her face is soft and full, with smooth pink cheeks and light-colored hair. She has the bluest eyes I've ever seen, but they are deep and distant. She is much younger than me. Her eyes are not.

Her deep eyes shine at me, and for a moment I feel as though I'm twelve years old again with little Emily Berchwitz at the Erie County Fair. In the evening, as the summer air cooled and the sounds of the fair seemed magical, Emily and I hid behind one of the arcade booths and ate cotton candy by the spinning light of a Ferris wheel.

Then I realize that what I smell is the lady's sugary breath, and I am suddenly sad to be here in the rain and not at a carnival. The lady seems very close to me. She is smiling and I have the urge to walk to work.

"Why are you looking at me?" I ask, avoiding her eyes.

"Do you own a cat?"

I take a full step back. "Yes, but—"

"I thought so." She turns away.

Now what? I wonder if there is cat hair on my suit. Is she able to smell cat? I think of Porky Pig cartoons where Sylvester would curl himself into a hat on Porky's head. I absently feel my head.

"I love cartoons," she says to the rain.

"What kind?" my mouth asks, to the surprise of my brain.

"All kinds. I like colors."

I consider the gray sky, my gray suit, my black shoes.

She steps forward into the rain, leaving her umbrella propped slightly on her shoulder. She looks up to the sky and her raincoat hood falls back, exposing long, blond hair, curled from the moisture. The rain soaks her face, her hair. She opens her mouth to collect the water.

I step toward her, closer to the edge of the shelter. I begin to reach out to the rain, when she drops her head.

"The rain's not for you," she says sadly. "Not today."

She steps back, leans against the far wall of the shelter and replaces her hood.

I try to watch her out of the corner of my eye. I wait for her to say something, unable to speak myself. I look for her to move, to act.

"Don't wait for me," she whispers.

My jaw drops. She is a sage, then, a suburban seer in plastic rain-gear. I wonder if her parlor is decorated with lava lamps and velvet paintings of tigers and purple landscapes. I envision a couch, long and high-backed, with huge brass buttons in the center of the cushions. The room is swarming with cats of all different sizes and colors. With a wave of their master's hand, the cats do the lady's bidding. She home brews ginseng tea and serves it to her guests on tiny porcelain saucers. House-wives and truck drivers come from miles around to hear her say things like, "Be careful with your money this weekend," and, "An important letter will be arriving soon."

"Your train is here," she says.

It's waiting for me. The ticket collector is standing there mildly annoyed. It takes me a second to remember I need to go to work. I realize the rain has stopped.

I hop on the train as it begins to move and run to the back. I open a window and shout, "What's your name?" The blue lady just smiles shyly and twirls her umbrella. The raindrops reflect off her shiny coat and the last thing I see before the train rounds a bend is a swirling, sky blue kaleidoscope.

Imagine the Universe Beautiful

HEAT WAVES RISE UP from the suburban lawn ornaments like tiny swaying spiderwebs. A pink flamingo, its head bent at an impossible angle, melted, hangs by a soft plastic thread.

The summer is so hot, the grass turns brown by mid-July. The children always come home with burned and blistering feet from skidding down the old metal slide at the end of Denaly Street. The slide is dangerously smooth, worn down from generations of young sliders. Sometimes, the metal gets so hot, some of the older kids light matches by holding them against the rail.

Danny has had enough of the playground, of the rusted swing's sweaty chains. He sits in the heat eating orange-vanilla popsicles on Mr. Keeler's front porch. The kid has the ice cream all over his face, dripping onto his hands and lap.

Danny's neighbor is in the habit of dragging out a small cherry-red cooler crammed full of popsicles. Every morning Mr. Keeler says the same thing.

"Hey Danny, how 'bout a popsicle? It'll cool ya off like an ice cube down your pants."

The boy is Mr. Keeler's favorite of the Denaly Street kids. The ten-year-old has freckled patches on his nose and thin, wiry arms and legs. He has a frazzled tuft of red and blond hair that reminds Mr. Keeler of a time when the older man didn't have to wear hats in the sun. The kid is out of a Sears and Roebuck painting, one of those cardboard jobs that shows poor kids with big eyes.

Danny is always hungry for popsicles, and downs two or three. Man and boy sit on two old, metal milk crates, fanning themselves, and offering popsicles to whomever happens by. Danny hands them out.

The boy's parents aren't around much; his father not at all. Danny was told his father wasn't coming back, that his father is now a woman named Marge in Las Vegas. Danny just figures his father is on a long vacation and will come home in a while. The tall, bald man in the robe had asked who Danny wanted to live with. The boy remembers his mother's smirk after Danny had picked her, like she had won something. Danny only picked her because Las Vegas sounded far away and cold. Now, mother has to work and Mr. Keeler is Danny's chum, at least for this summer.

There's a pause in the popsicle-giving. Danny watches the sidewalk, the yellowing row of houses across the way, practically clamped together like Legos. The street is as quiet as a sigh.

"Have you ever been to the gate, Danny?" Mr. Keeler asks.

"What gate?"

And then, for the better part of the afternoon, Mr. Keeler tells him. He tells Danny of the old paper mill down in the valley, back behind Danny's house. He tells him of the generations of families, including his own, who have lived in its shadow, endured its noise and smell.

"You think them old railroad tracks smell bad now, Danny?" he says, tweaking his nose between his thumb and forefinger. "Well, you should have smelled that old sawmill. Sometimes, there would rise above the trees, behind your house and mine, a cloud of sawdust and tar so big it would block out the sun."

Danny looks at the tree line behind his house and tries to imagine a monster dust cloud shaped perhaps like a grizzly bear or a witch, like the one in *The Wizard of Oz*.

The woods behind Danny and Mr. Keeler's house smell of pine in the summer and rust in the winter. He has a hard time negotiating the long-abandoned railroad tracks that run through the valley. During the summer, the tracks are difficult to find because he gets lost in the weeds and shrubs. In fall, though, the smell of rotting steel and rusty spikes is unmistakable. Then Danny can find the tracks easily and follow them for a hundred yards or perhaps two hundred, before running home with images of hobos and trolls chasing him away.

Mr. Keeler tells Danny of how a disaster destroyed the paper mill many years before Danny was born. He points to the dent in the roof of his tool shed. A chunk of metal from the explosion had sailed nearly a mile before coming to rest on the shed. Then, he tells Danny about the only part of the paper mill still standing, its iron gate.

There's no sleep for Danny tonight. He can't wrap his head around the idea of the gate and the sawmill. It's too big. He stays awake, his sheets damp from the heat, his eyes stinging from sweat, his fear in his throat.

Only two walls separate the boy from Mr. Keeler. The man's house is dark, save the blue glow from the television. Keeler stands in his kitchen, looking out into the hot night, looking out into a past that's as faded as paint in the sun.

As faded as the flag that's framed in Keeler's living room, a white flag with a single orange circle in the center. In the white silk several small holes form perfect circles. The silk around the holes is chalky red from the blood of the soldier Keeler killed. Killed and then took his flag, a flag that the soldier grasped in death.

Keeler sits in front of the television, studies the photos on the tube, by the fireplace, on the mantel. He wears loose-fitting boxer shorts; the edge of his stomach creeps just above the waistband.

Keeler was sixty-seven when the kid was born. Now Keeler is old, but his eyes are sharp, his legs are sturdy like a horse's. Keeler keeps fit by walking the rails, the same rails he'll take Danny over tomorrow.

Keeler's arms are tight and drawn like beef jerky. The scars on his shoulder, on his knee and behind his left ear were all received in Okinawa. Keeler touches the white streak by his ear where a bullet whizzed through and thinks of the years between the war and now.

Of his marriage to Maureen, of his two children who died long before their father. He thinks of the mill. He remembers how the ground feels when it moves underfoot. He feels a touch of vertigo and grasps the arms of his soft chair.

Then Keeler is running as the earth shakes underneath. He feels the bricks tumbling and a smokestack falling. He sees the massive pair of black gates, the portal that will save him.

He thinks nothing of the men who fall around him, of the blood. He's seen blood before, caused blood to run. Now, it's just his life. Everything is just his life. The gates meant life then.

And now, the gates are the end. Finally the end.

The next morning, Danny sees Mr. Keeler first. The man has brown walking boots tied tightly against khaki overalls. Underneath is an already sweat-stained white T-shirt. On his head, an old baseball cap: Brooklyn Dodgers. His hard, brown fingers play across the cap's rim like he's a pitcher giving signals. He stands on his porch, one leg up on the rail, like an explorer, like Lewis or Clark—Danny remembers them from last spring's history lesson.

Mr. Keeler turns and sees Danny. There's no smile and no popsicles.

"Are you ready, my boy?"

Danny nods furiously.

"I'm ready, sir!" Danny has never called Mr. Keeler sir. Never called anyone that.

They set off, Mr. Keeler slightly ahead. There is morning dew, but it will soon be boiled off by the sun. Behind the boy's and man's yards are the woods, into which they burst, caring little for the burrs and vines encountered along the way. Danny has rarely been here during the summer. The woods are thick and they smell of pine. Dry dirt and sap surround the two explorers. It takes Danny three steps for every one of Mr. Keeler's. They don't talk much.

Mr. Keeler crashes through the brush like a bulldozer. Danny can only look up at the man's wide back. Mr. Keeler's powerful red hands push tree limbs aside. His huge boots stomp out a path. Thorns and burrs cling to the man's pants and T-shirt and he brushes them off like flies. Mr. Keeler is confident and in his element. He is a totally different man from the one who eats popsicles on his porch. Every so often he looks back at Danny and hands the boy some nuts or corn bread from an apparently bottomless pocket. Sometimes he just gives the boy a wink. Danny can't remember if his father ever winked at him, but he thinks of his father anyway.

Then, with the suddenness of a lightning bolt, they are in a clearing. Danny marches up next to Mr. Keeler and sees why they have stopped. They have found the tracks. There are weeds and bushes and small trees sprouting from under and between the rocks and splintered ties and tarnished steel rails. Danny knows the tracks. To his right is an endless horizon leading out of his town. To his left is the valley and the sawmill. That's the direction they head in.

They mount the abandoned tracks and Mr. Keeler finally speaks. "Down that way, Danny," he points to the right, "is Manchester. That's where I was born."

Danny tries to imagine Manchester, fails, then instead tries to imagine Mr. Keeler as a boy. Danny sees jet black hair, which never touches young Mr. Keeler's ears, thick calves and dark purposeful eyes; Mr. Keeler with all the hopes and dreams of any young man. Danny looks at his summer friend and sees a boy under the wrinkles and leather skin.

Mr. Keeler sits down on one of the hot rails and unfastens a canvas pouch from his belt, a pouch Danny didn't see till now. The water sack's cork makes a loud, wet "pop" that seems to shake the trees. "Break time," Mr. Keeler says and takes a long, noisy draft, the liquid drifting lazily down his red cheek. "Ahhhh . . ." He flips off his cap and wipes his glistening forehead in the same motion. "Did you ever drink whiskey, Danny?"

"Sure!" The only time Danny has even heard the word whiskey was from one of the older boys at the park. Or from mother.

Mr. Keeler laughs and passes the sack. "Take it slow, son. It will burn at first."

And it does. Danny chokes, then coughs and coughs and coughs till his eyes water and his fingertips are numb and he feels like he's on a roller coaster ride with a 200-foot drop. After a minute of Mr. Keeler's hard back-slaps, Danny manages to croak, "It's good!"

Then Mr. Keeler laughs again, harder this time. Soon Danny joins in and they are both holding their bellies and roaring like two lions in the deepest jungle of Africa.

Life has no meaning for Keeler and all the meaning at the same time. He is in the hospital for three weeks after the explosion and fire. On his stomach. His wounds are deep, slicing through his back like a million razors. The white slashes are brighter than the bullet scar.

He can't see them. His wife describes them. She traces her finger over them, lightly. The gesture causes some pain for Keeler but he wants to know, wants to feel the physical pain like he feels the pain in his head and his heart.

Maureen sits at his bedside, but neither talks much. The wounds separate them like a pane of glass. Keeler's back is scarred, not his chest and not his face. He had his back to the explosion, to the men he worked with who struggled to escape. Some went back in to help others and did not return.

But the wounds are only on Keeler's back. Maureen knows this. He can see it in her face, in her pale face, her once blue eyes now gray and distant.

By noon, the explorers have gone far beyond any boundaries Danny has ever explored by himself. They have seen a deer and Danny has found, along with forty-two cents in loose change, a heavy track spike that has been painted gold.

The boy's fear begins to fade. There are no hobos or monsters this time. There is only the sun, which beats down on Danny's shoulders. There is only Mr. Keeler, his legs pumping like pistons, breathing heavy but steady.

They have come to the factory and are standing on the edge of the tracks looking down a sharp decline. Past the edge of the forest, however, are not more trees, but stone foundations and rotten wood crisscrossing every which way. There is glass everywhere, smoke-stained and pitted from fire and years of rain and winter. The ruins seem endless.

This is what remains of the factory. In his mind Danny tries to recreate the images placed there by Mr Keeler: the huge paper mill, surrounded by men, like carpenter ants hurrying in and around the plant. Hundreds of booted feet, every day, as though it were the marching of all these men that sunk the factory deep into the valley. Steam and soot rise from endless rows of chimney stacks. The sound is deep and organized, and Danny almost feels it reverberating in his chest. Then, like the explosion that ended the factory's life, the boy's vision is ended by Mr. Keeler's firm grip on his shoulder.

"This is it," he is saying slowly as though in a dream, "this is it. Not much different."

Danny takes a deep breath and feels the sweat dripping from his forehead and chin. He reaches out with the tip of his tongue and tastes the salt in his sweat. He feels suddenly angry, wishing for a home baseball team and a father to take him to a game. He wants mother to read to him again. He looks up at Mr. Keeler, who looks out over the ruins with deep eyes, squinting just slightly in the sun. Danny wonders if father ever looked at something like that. Further, Danny wonders if he'll ever look at something like that. Mr. Keeler looks out over his past with fury.

Sgt. Keeler shot the fleeing Jap in the back. Shot him dead, like an animal, then laughed about it later to his men. Shot him in the back, then in the chest as his enemy cried and begged some unknown God for mercy.

And Sgt. Keeler shot him dead and took the flag.

"Shall we pass through, Danny?" Mr. Keeler's voice is steady, but suddenly sad. The boy is ready.

They climb down into the valley. Here there are no trees, ivy or thorns: only ruins, silent testimony of man once again being repelled by nature or fate or perhaps a little of both. Danny walks over broken stone and bent steel. The sun doesn't seem to shine so brightly here. The collapsed mill is simply a larger pile of rubble than the surrounding piles, which used to be shops and sheds. Waste, identifiable only by the memory of what it once was; mounds of wood and metal that used to represent progress and power, now only acres of dead, dusty concrete.

Danny doesn't care about the ruins outside the main mill because he can see it now, the gate: giant black bars, pointed at the top like hundreds of Indian arrowheads. The iron barrier is still standing. It sags in some spots where the ground below has caved in, but it is still very much intact.

The gate rises up before him, still determined to protect the mill. There are two huge iron pillars, each topped with a tremendous ball on a pedestal. There is an archway from one black ball to the next. In the archway, a pattern is still visible; two trees, their branches wrapped lovingly around an image of the mill. Danny shivers. The trees on the archway seem angry. He wonders if, maybe, the trees blew up the mill. He looks down quickly.

Suddenly, Danny understands what happened to this place and he becomes afraid of a past that ended swiftly, in fire and pain, like the pain Father Raymond describes in such detail every Sunday. This pain, according to the priest, is inevitable unless Danny is able to feel sorry for his sins. Danny looks around and wonders how many men had felt sorry for their sins the day their world ceased to exist. He wonders if, as their mill was exploding around them, they had time to think about anything else besides saving their lives. Finally, Danny wonders if God will forgive those who died with thoughts of self-preservation on their mind instead of forgiveness, or if that brief deviation from faith condemned them eternally.

Keeler feels the white hot burn on his back. Pieces of his dark blue work shirt fry into his skin. He yells out, but no one hears over the fire and the screams of the other men.

Cinders and ash, chunks of concrete and sliver-sharp arrows of iron and brick rain overhead. He stumbles once, catches himself with his right hand, breaking four bones just above the knuckle in the process, but doesn't feel it.

He tries to step over the dark figure of a man but another explosion shakes the earth and Keeler falls into the man instead of over him.

The man grunts, opens his eyes, looks to Keeler for help. Keeler pushes on instead. He charges through the gate, his world on fire, and keeps running until he falls in a heap at the door of his own home.

Danny feels Mr. Keeler's arm around his shoulders, the man pushing the boy forward just slightly. Danny feels the woods and the sun and the wind and the cold concrete under his feet. He looks through the gate and sees his whole life stretched before him.

The kid looks up at Mr. Keeler for answers, for direction, but Keeler is seeing something else, something long past. Keeler is imagining the world a more beautiful place.

"Are you ready, son?" he asks, not looking down at the boy.

Danny nods.

A warm breeze falls from the distant trees just then and Danny and Mr. Keeler feel its caress at their backs as the two explorers, man and boy, pass through the gate.

Sing

FROM INSIDE THE DARK CLOSET I hear him slap Laura, probably with the back of his hand. She makes a sound like "oh!."

That's my cue.

I check the gun belt and make sure I'm not hooked on any of her clothes. The closet is full of glittering things that smell like her. My entrance must be dramatic. I kick the double doors open and shatter the flimsy knob that pops off the door and skitters across the floor into a dark corner. I didn't mean to do that, but the added drama will likely earn me an extra couple bucks. I step forward into the light of a single standing lamp and am able to evaluate the situation.

Laura is tied to a wooden post in the middle of a bare room near the center of the ring of light. Her hands are strapped together behind the slab like in the movies. Her feet are tied together, but in front of her so she can stand. There are some ropes around her waist, but they don't look tight. She's wearing a cheerleader outfit, blue and white, like the Dallas Cowgirls only tighter. It looks like satin and it shimmers like crystal as she struggles against the phony ropes.

Her face is thick with eyeliner and rouge, her fake lashes ridiculously long. Her hair, red and yellow, is like fire. Laura sucks the air out of any room she's in.

The guy who slapped her is just like all the others; over weight, mid-fifties and sweating. He's dressed as a Nazi, right down to the swastika arm bands. I wonder briefly if the outfit is his, or Laura's. He turns to look at me when I come out of the closet and I realize he's quite a bit taller than I had expected. Usually, the ones that pick Nazis are small, trying to overcompensate. I learn later that he didn't know I was coming—I'm a little extra something from Laura to one of her favorites.

Nazis and cheerleaders. It's always the same.

Everything so far has been scripted. From this point, I'm on my own.

"Just what in the hell is going on here," I slur, not quite sure whether a Clint Eastwood or Rambo accent is more appropriate for the situation.

I'm wearing high Army boots, and camouflage pants with a beige muscle T-shirt. I have two rows of bullets strung across my chest, though they aren't real. I have two guns, one a German Luger, the other a 9 mm Glock. Those are real, but not loaded. I don't feel that either fit my character, but what the hell. The Luger was the right choice anyway.

Slowly, I pull on a pair of heavy black gloves, leather padded around the knuckles.

The guy is tall, but he begins to fold up into himself. He knows what's coming, but I don't let him prepare too much.

I step forward, into my punch, and throw my weight behind an upward right cross. I hit him, just under his left eye, making certain not to break his nose. I was told earlier that it's okay if I break his cheek bone.

It's a closed fist punch, and I don't want to crack my knuckles so I pull a little, not so he'd notice. I land solidly enough, knuckles straight on just under the eye socket, and he goes down like a sack of wet rags.

"You okay little lady," I ask Laura, falling into a John Wayne slur.

"He hurt me." She winks. "Please don't hurt me."

I look down at the Nazi. My punch opened up a small cut

under his eye. I knocked his hat off and I notice that his thinning hair doesn't quite cover his balding head. He clutches my leg and pulls himself up, gasping.

Before he's able to get completely to his feet, I kick him in the groin and he goes down again. I step back to reevaluate.

His cheek is swollen, but it doesn't look like I broke any bones. The groin shot will smart for a while, but I'm not wearing steel toes so nothing serious there. He sucks air like a fish for a couple minutes before he starts to get his feet under him. I just stand there waiting, looking down on him, keeping a straight face. I wish he would stay down.

"Please," he says to me, "please don't hurt me."

But he's smiling.

I feel sick. He's on his knees now, so I reach down and pull him to his feet by his left hand pinkie finger. I pull him close to my face, till I can smell his sour breath.

"This'll teach you," I hiss.

With my right hand I exert pressure on his finger. With my left hand I grab his crotch. When I feel how sickeningly hard he is, I really do get angry and twist his finger like a bottlecap.

He groans, and I give his pinkie one final turn. The pop of the breaking bone echoes like a firecracker in the emptiness of the room.

"Yes!" he cries the moment the bone snaps, and he passes out. I drop him quickly, untie Laura, and go to the bathroom to wash my hands.

Later, Laura and I are sipping coffee at a deli down the street from her flat. The air outside is razor sharp and sizzles when it hits the deli windows. Everywhere is dark.

"Look Michael, if you're so unhappy, then why do it?"

I shrug. "Gotta work. Besides, you asked." I hate it when she asks me questions she knows the answers to.

"Do you always do what your friends ask."

"Sure."

She shakes her head and reaches across the table to pat my cheek like you would a child even though we're the same age. Her palm smells like leather and soap.

"You're sweet. And you are a good friend. And, I don't think you hate it."

She made $5,000 from the Nazi. She slides an envelope across the table, which I know has my $1,000 cut. It's sealed. It's cash. I don't bother opening it. I just slip it into my coat pocket.

"One of those guys will hurt you," I tell her for no good reason. None of her clients will hurt her. I just feel like arguing.

"Not with you in my closet." She laughs, and without the makeup and eyelashes, she's beautiful. Laura's red hair sits on her shoulders, like she's giving it a ride. When she's working she pulls it back in a severe manner befitting her professional status.

Slight crow's feet are just beginning to show at the sides of her blue eyes.

"I'm not always in your closet."

She sighs. "You really are worried about me."

"Yes."

"I don't let them tie me up unless I have somebody there. Usually *I* tie *them* up. You know that."

Outside, the sleet has turned to rain and a mist has begun to settle over the rotting storefronts that dot Elm Street making Manchester look as old and angry as it actually is. It's late and the few pedestrians milling about outside all take cover in the deli. The bells above the door jangle endlessly.

"He's not really a Nazi, you know," she says, trying to be reassuring. "He works at a bank."

"He's lonely and small," I say.

"Maybe. He has a wife and three children. He loves them."

Before I can respond, Laura looks at her watch.

"Damn, I have a midnight. I have to go."

She bends over and kisses me on the forehead, then is gone. I watch until she disappears into the haze.

An hour later I'm sitting in my car in front of the Nazi's house. It's a cozy little Cape Cod in a cul-de-sac just outside the city. Earlier, I had copied down his address from Laura's client book.

He has a family. God knows how people like him explain the bruises and broken bones. I suppose they can justify the sessions as not being sex. Laura doesn't actually sleep with any of them, she just breaks them. Mostly, I break them I guess.

I sit in my car for a while, listening to the rain, feeling the heat pumping from the dashboard vents, letting my knuckles grow white on the steering wheel. Sometimes, after a job, my skin tingles for hours. Pins and needles.

I wait until it feels as though my flesh is literally crawling over my bones, then step out into the rain and walk over to his car, a silver Lexus. He's left it on the street even though there's a garage. I suppose he didn't want to wake the family.

I peek inside. It's alarmed but it makes no difference for my purposes. It's late and the weather is bad so the street is quiet. I slide a small pair of wire cutters out of a leather pouch I keep under my arm, and use it to snap off all four tire stems. I can hear the sound of the escaping air over the pouring rain, the air leaking onto the wet pavement like blood.

For the past year, I've lived with a girl named Mona Brand. She's nineteen now. She needed a place, she liked mine, she moved in.

She works as an usher at the Palace Theatre about two blocks away from where I bus tables and we often walk to work together. Sometimes we hold hands. Usually we just walk.

Mona's fine. She knows what I do and doesn't mind. In fact, she's actively interested in the way that girls her age mostly are, but I try to keep it away from her.

Mona and I slept together once, about a week after we met. Then, not long after that, Mona got us tickets to the Sesame Street on Ice show and she got high beforehand and kept telling people she wanted to fight Grover, and Grover was spying on her. It was funny, but after that I didn't want to sleep with her anymore.

We have separate rooms now.

On the way to work the afternoon after the Nazi, Mona asked me what I thought about Brad. Brad is a basketball player, a black guy, who Mona has been having loud sex with for the last month. I know nothing else about him, though they occasionally knock books off my shelves and I sometimes find a basketball in the hallway.

"He has a manly voice," I say.

She laughs. "I mean, do you like him?"

"I don't know him."

"But do you like him?"

"He's tall."

"He asked about you the other day."

I look down at Mona, who's at least a foot shorter than I am. Mona dyed her hair black about a week ago, but looking down on the top of her head I can see a few dirty blond spots that she missed. She has studs in her eye lids, nose, ears, mouth, tongue and a bunch of other places not normally displayed in public. Piercings are immature.

"If there were a war, they'd have to melt you for ammunition," I say.

"Come on, I'm serious."

I'm a little ticked that she apparently told him about me.

"I don't take on black guys."

"Why not?"

"I just don't."

We walk a few blocks. It's early winter, and Manchester

smells cold and moldy. It's more conversation than I've had with Mona since I met her.

"What is he looking for?" I ask.

"Not sure if it's him or some guy on his team."

"Another black guy?"

"They're basketball players."

Mona digs around in her purse, comes back out with a business card and hands it to me.

"This is the woman he's with. He said to call."

The card says Frost. There's a phone number.

"What kind of name is that?" I ask.

"Beats me. That's her name."

"Never heard of her."

"So don't call her."

I slip the paper in my pocket. Rain is coming and we walk the rest of the way in silence.

The restaurant I bus for is called Italian Delight. I don't need the money, but it's something to do. My boss is a guy named Pete, and sometimes after work he'll gather a bunch of us together for some Poker. Pete smokes pot, and he often offers me some as we stand in the alley during a break.

"Fucks up the body, Pete," I tell him.

Pete's a big guy, and by that I mean fat. He's greasy and has huge, red, puffy hands.

"My body's already fucked up," he says. It is, too. Pete is going to die soon. I tell him as much. He just shrugs.

I don't drink. I don't smoke. If I'm not working, I'm running. Mostly, I'm bored. Pete's okay though. He looks out for us busboys, and waiters too. I often take home leftover food, though I only eat pasta, not pizza. I usually work the late shift, maybe twenty-five or thirty hours a week. I have nothing else to do during the week. I like working at night, when it's cool and people have fewer inhibitions. I've picked up some work by just being around at night. It's got to a point where I just let it come to me now.

Nobody ever talks about it to my face, except maybe Laura or Mona. People always beat around the bush, like they want to hire me to cut their lawn.

For example, a couple months age, this scrawny little Guido is sitting in a booth by the window all night, barely eating and just sipping a Coke. I can tell he's not local. For two hours, he's rubbing his hands, looking at me, rubbing his hands, looking at me. I know what he wants, but it's up to him. I finally go over to collect his plates and sweep up, and he says to me, "Are you Michael? Do you do *work*?"

"Yeah, I bus tables."

"No, other work." He doesn't look at me.

"What kind of work you have in mind."

"Easy."

"Tell me what you are looking for."

He scribbles some words down on a napkin and hands it to me. It reads, "I want you to burn me." There is a phone number.

"You go through anyone?"

"What do you mean?"

"I don't do direct work. You have to go through someone."

"What, but I thought—"

I cut him off. "We're done."

I'm a contractor, yes, but not a private contractor. I never work directly with the client, only through established locals like Laura. And even then, the mild work they do themselves. Usually that only amounts to a little bit of bondage and some bruises. But often, when it's about blood and broken bones, I get the nod. I'm good at what I do and my reputation gets around. Precision is key, going far enough but not too far takes a professional.

So, a week later I get a call from some dungeon master in

Bedford named Rick who wants to know if I can do some work on a little client. Turns out it's the scrawny guy.

We meet, Rick and I, to talk about the client's needs, but also to make sure we're comfortable with each other. Turns out the scrawny guy is right. It's easy. It takes me five minutes to singe the hair off his chest and blacken his nipples with a propane torch. I make $500.

So now, when I'm at work, I keep my eyes open.

Later in the week, I'm in Portsmouth watching TV at Jullian's house when he starts up with me.

"How come you don't play anymore, Michael?"

"Don't have a piano." I'm annoyed two seconds into the conversation. On my days off, I try to visit my brother. He's respectable. He has cable. He has a house with ivy growing up the side. He has a Wacky Water Wheely in his backyard. He has a kid, my nephew, Jack.

My brother has won awards. He has won elections. He's a jackass though.

"You make enough. You could buy one," he says.

I don't say anything. I just channel surf.

"I talked to Pop the other day," he says.

I come across one of those infomercials, this one selling a thing called the Bow-Flex. It's all strung out with ties and levers. I'm a big fan of wires and pulleys. It looks like something Laura might use for work.

Jullian is still talking. "He asked about you. I told him you were doing fine. I told him you were playing again."

"What? Why did you tell him that?"

"What, I'm going to tell him what you really do?"

My brother thinks he knows what I do, but he doesn't have the full picture.

"You don't have to tell him anything," I say.

Jullian's wife walks in then and the conversation ends. I

watch Jullian kiss Amy. They whisper a while, probably about me, and Amy disappears into the kitchen.

"Stay for dinner," Jullian says.

"No."

"You come all the way here and you won't stay for dinner?"

"Yes."

He shrugs. "Suit yourself."

Jullian is a dentist. He's been married for eight years. I mainly work the Merrimack Valley, but some of my richest scores have come from yuppies who live in Portsmouth.

Money does something to people, makes them think life is about danger and excitement. It makes them want to try new things instead of just buying a flat-screen TV and staying the hell home. Mostly what it leads to is fucking up your rich life.

It's why I'm glad Jullian is happy with the house and the boat which he takes out into the harbor a couple times a year. I'm even glad he's happy with Amy, even though she's a controlling troll.

Jullian is two years younger than me, though we both have similar features—sunken eyes, black hair, a rigid chin. I'm in much better shape and I'm sure this bothers Amy.

I hear her clanging around in the kitchen. She doesn't like my being here, in *their* house. I'm a stain on their perfect life, a stick of dynamite that could pop and there goes the white picket fence. Jullian says that he never speaks with her about what I do, but she's afraid of me.

Break enough bones and you're able to get a strong sense for people real fast. On the day of their wedding, during the reception, I managed to get Amy alone for a few minutes. I told her that if she ever broke my brother's heart or did anything but make him happy, I would snap every one of her knuckles on all her fingers. I also told her that if my brother discovered that we had this conversation, I would burn down her parents' home.

I have her number.

"Why don't you visit Pop?" Jullian is saying.

"No vacation time." I smile.

"He's not well, you know."

"What now?'

"His knees are bad. I was talking to him yesterday, and he can't hear."

"He's old."

"You should visit."

My father worked in a steel mill for fifty-three years. By the time he retired, mom was dead and all my father had to show for all his years of labor was a beat-up two-story on one measly acre of land in upstate New York and a pair of red, callused hands. Well, and Jullian, I guess. Jullian makes nearly as much as me.

"You're the one he's proud of," I tell Jullian.

Jullian is quiet for a moment, then he mumbles, "Still, you should visit."

My childhood house was a two-story box built by my father and his three brothers. They labored for one whole summer, shipping material in from distant Lackawanna. Old yellowing photos show my dad, glistening in the sun, bare-chested, giving directions to my uncles. Another photo shows my father carrying Mom in front of their half-built house, thinking, I imagine, that their whole life is in front of them, that it will always be that good.

Turns out my mother actually had the cancer then, though she wouldn't know it for fifteen years.

Now, the house is just a shell, the white paint replaced by rust and dirt. My father is too old to maintain the yard so the place is a jungle. There's a Quick Stop that never closes across the street from my old bedroom window and the red and green neon sign lights up the room twenty-four seven. The street itself has been upgraded and widened and widened again to make room for the faceless boxes. There's a parking lot to the left and to the right of the old house. My father's acre spreads out behind the house, only about fifty feet wide, but extending back into a jangle of scrubs and trees and a small creek that, somehow, miraculously, has remained undeveloped and still courses behind the strip malls.

I haven't been here in three years, but it all looks the same and it all looks different. My foot goes straight through the second step as I climb the back-porch stairs. The step collapses into rot and termites.

"Watch that step," my father says from the porch. "It's a doozy."

He's been sitting there watching me. The porch is enclosed but it's still cold. He's wearing a parka and sitting in a lime green lawn chair. He's holding a rubber mallet.

"What're you doing, Pop?"

"Watching for moles," he says.

"Find any?"

He shakes his head. "But when I do . . ." he trails off, but swings the mallet down to show me how those moles are going to suffer. "Want some tea?"

Before I can answer, he shuffles off into the house, leaving the door open for me. He's wearing rubber galoshes, and walks with a stoop I never noticed before. I follow him into the kitchen.

The whole house rattles as a truck roars past outside.

I'm not interested in playing nice.

"Sell this place, Pop," I say.

"You want sugar," he asks knowing I do.

"Look at that outside," I say peering through the dusty curtains. "This isn't even a neighborhood anymore. You're living on a highway."

For years, my father has slammed the door and ripped up the letters of every developer who ever wanted to erect a Stop and Go. His little one acre might as well be a pot of gold.

"Home is home," he says quietly. He runs his hand over the top of his bald scalp, closing his eyes for a moment.

"Home is a strip mall, Pop—"

He snaps. "Stop! Tell me to sell my home once more and I will smash your skull in with this teapot!"

He picks up the pot and shakes it at me. Tea splashes onto the linoleum floor. We're both quiet for a moment. I get some paper towels and clean the spill while he pours us each a cup of what's left.

Later that week, I finally meet Frost. She's tall, well over six-foot and much of it is legs. She has white hair, like a horse's mane, and she has silver eyes. I'm certain they are contacts, but the look is wicked. The reason I never heard of her, she tells me as we walk through her place in Cambridge, is because she does very selective work, one job, maybe two a year.

She has a vaguely European accent, but it might be fake.

Frost's apartment is expensive; four rooms downstairs, three upstairs, two bathrooms and an attic which she does not take me through. I assume that's where her playrooms are. My decision to work through people like Frost as opposed to actually doing the work myself has a lot to do with space. Mona and I share a five-room double on the second floor. I like it because Mona pays half the rent and I'm a short walk away from Laura's place.

Since I work mainly as a private contractor, I only need equipment, not space. My apartment building has an attic area where I keep my costumes, and equipment. The rest is mine. Mona and I share a bathroom but other than that we get along just fine. I don't have to worry about chains on walls, and lighting and all that other crap. I come in, do my business and I'm done for the day. I don't even have to clean up any messes after.

But Frost's place is different. It's the big league. Time and resources are invested here that can only exist, in her line of work, if some of her clients are cops and elected officials.

She has paintings on her walls—Picasso, Warhol. They look real, but I only glance at them. There is a shelf with some African looking statues and tribal masks. I see no books.

"How do you manage to have this apartment only doing one or two clients a year?"

"Condo dear. I own it. I told you, my work is *special*."

"Then why do you need me?"

"Normally I wouldn't dear, but Brad, my client, asked for you by name."

We sit in her living room on a soft white couch that is barely more than a bunch of huge cushions. She pours herself Champagne. I drink water.

"Brad is one of my favorites," she begins.

"Why?"

She laughs. "He's rich, dear. Filthy rich. The son of a publisher."

Okay, so it's a profit thing for her. I can deal with that.

"At any rate, let's get acquainted," she says. "Take off your shirt."

I do. What do I care?

"You keep yourself fit. Nice. Steroids?"

"No."

"Good for you. Now, you."

"Me what?"

"Ask me a question, we'll take turns."

"I'm not interested, Frost."

"Ah, right to business eh?"

"No, I'm just not interested enough in you." I put my shirt back on.

She looks at me for a few seconds, then sighs.

"Brad plays basketball at a weekend jock club in Boston. He

and some of his teammates combine their resources once a year and come to me to pass the time."

"I see."

"Oh, don't be judgmental, dear. That's not what I expected from you. It must get so boring for those little boys, being rich and all."

"The point."

"The point, is that this year is special. This year Brad wants something only for himself that I have never been able to offer."

"And that is?"

"Something you've never done, Michael." Frost leans forward and slides her hand up my thigh. She leans in close till her lips brush my ear. "Something terribly exciting. Something just for you."

Laura is talking to me about her day, but I'm tuned out. I keep looking at her hair, but thinking about Frost.

"Michael, what is it?" Laura finally asks.

We're at Home Depot looking for rope. Occasionally, as we walk, Laura will put her arm around my waist or direct me with a hand on my elbow. I wonder if passing shoppers think we're a couple.

I'm reminded of a trip she and I took to Montreal back before we worked. We strolled arm in arm through the busy streets at the height of that city's annual jazz festival. But in the midst of all that noise, Laura heard a piano. She dragged me down a crumbling set of steps into a lower basement cafe. No signs, no tourist menu on some delicate entrance way.

The place was dank and tiny—single bar, a half dozen stools. It smelled like cellar hole musk and cheap cigarettes. In an unlit corner was a stand-up baby grand, so damaged by water and mold that the wooden hood was warped. The ivory keys were green and greasy.

And old black man sat on a rotting stool just tinkering, play-ing chopsticks one second and Thelonious Monk the next. He looked up when we approached. When he saw Laura he just got up and walked away. I remember that the most. It was like he had been tuning that damn piano for her and had just been awaiting her arrival.

She sat right down and started to play, just moving her del-icate fingers over the bloated keys. Time stood still. Her face, nearly a silhouette against a pitch black wall, like an etching, seemed to stop in time for me. She disappeared that day for a few minutes, just left the room, the world, herself. Just went inside someplace.

When she came back to me, after what seemed like hours, but was probably only a few minutes, she patted the seat. I slid down next to her and began to play, not really having anything in mind, but surprised when the melody came and she began to sing.

"Blow, ill wind, blow away, let me rest today, you're blowin' me no good . . ."

She sang with a slight lilt, channeling Billie Holiday, but mostly just being herself. I played, and she sang and not a single tourist of the millions that walked above us walked through those doors. The black man swept behind the dark bar, the oily piano keys felt like velvet and I convinced myself in those few moments that this was to be my life.

"Michael," Laura is asking again. "Come on back to me. What's wrong?"

"Nothing, I'm fine."

The bruise on Laura's cheek has faded.

"You haven't been yourself lately," she says. "Why haven't you come around?"

I haven't felt myself, I think.

"Busy."

"What, at the restaurant?" Laura laughs and I laugh with her because her teeth are so bright against her deep red lips.

"No, busy with work."

This is true, though I've never had work like this. I am concerned with detail; who are my clients, who is their family, how much money do they make, do I have contingencies if something goes wrong? I make a point of never taking a job without doing research first.

For the last week, I have researched Frost. And found next to nothing. The tax rolls in Cambridge list Frost's condo as being owned by S. Frost. S. Frost paid her property taxes last year and her condo is valued at $650,000. She bought the condo seven years ago. That's it.

No one on the street has heard of her.

"Have you ever heard of Frost?" I ask Laura.

"A client?"

"Possibly."

"Like me?" She's preoccupied with rope, testing different lengths, stretching them out and running her fingers over the different textures.

"No, nothing at all like you."

After a few moments, Laura returns her attention to me. "Never heard of him."

"Her."

She shrugs. "Is that why you haven't come around?"

"Partly. It's a pretty big job I'm looking into."

"Well, good. You're good at what you do." She unexpectedly kisses me on the lips.

"Why did you do that?" I feel angry suddenly, but it passes in a moment.

"Felt like it."

"Do you always do what you feel like?" I ask, knowing the answer.

She doesn't hear, as I am no longer the center of her universe.

Frost may not exist, but Brad does. He is the son of Max Thornton, a stockbroker in Boston. Mr. Thornton owns a minor-league baseball team, has a place out on Marblehead. He probably has brandy with other businessmen at some yacht club in the bay. He has two children, Brad and someone called Boxey. I don't know if Boxey is a boy or a girl, but that doesn't matter.

It appears that Brad does nothing except be the son of a wealthy person.

Yesterday, nearly a week after my conversation with Frost, Brad breaches the subject with me while I search the fridge for something to eat. It's 2:00 a.m. He's just fucked Mona and is in a puffed-up alpha-male mood. He's wearing a towel. His chest is shaved, and damp with sweat.

"Put a shirt on," I tell him.

He looks at me like I'm a bug.

"Look, it's been a week. You going to take the job or what?"

It's a breach of . . . something, for him to bring this up. He steps over a line.

I lean back against the counter. "Why are you here, Brad?"

"What do you mean? I'm hungry."

"No, I mean why are you in this apartment, in this city, fucking this girl?" I speak slowly like he's retarded. "A rich, well-bred boy like you—a black boy speaking like a white boy, slumming it. Must be better tail out there, penthouses someplace you can get a better view from."

He's silent for a moment, then decides I'm kidding with him, like maybe one of his rich pals might. He laughs, but there's uncertainty now.

"Look, dude, you can make a quarter of million bucks here. That must mean something to a guy like you."

"Don't call me dude."

"What's with you? This is what you do right? So fucking do it."

He pops open a quart of milk and puts it to his lips. A drop of sweat rolls off his forehead and into the carton.

I punch him in the stomach, just below the sternum.

It's a quick jab, little more than a tap, but he's not prepared for it. He goes down, spitting up some milk in the process. He's coughing and sputtering and trying to cover himself with his towel.

I take my time, like I might with a client. He wants to fight, but he knows he can't. I squat down in front of him, eye level. He's sucking wind.

"Brad, what I just did, that's what I do. What you are asking of me, I have never done. Now, I'm going to take some time to think about it and I'll let Frost know."

I decide to take a walk. On the way out I pass Mona who has watched the whole episode. She doesn't say anything, but I can't see any fear in her eyes.

Frost is sitting on her sofa, her long legs under her, like a cat. She is sipping something red. Her fingernails are silver, along with her hair and her eyes. She strokes my inner thigh as we talk. I can't get a fix on her age. Older than me, maybe early forties, but she could just as well be twenty or sixty.

"I've heard so much about you Michael, so many good things."

"From who?"

"Whom, dear, whom," she corrects me. "Just people, clients, talk on the street."

"From what I can tell, you've never been on the streets. Who are you?"

She laughs. "I'm no different than you Michael. A bit more discreet perhaps."

111

"I never hide who I am or what I do. Here or anywhere."

She stares at me a long time, then leans over and kisses me. I taste wine on her lips. It's a good kiss.

"Who would you tell about that kiss. Your mother?"

"My mother is dead."

"Mother, father, who cares. You know what I mean."

"I would tell anyone what I want."

"What won't hurt them, you mean. Or hurt you, perhaps?"

I'm quiet.

"Anyway, dear, I'm glad you came. Brad told me that you gave him a little . . . sample the other night."

"I hit him."

"Such a ruffian. Well, he's practically going out of his mind with anticipation. He wants an answer."

"I haven't made up my mind."

Frost sighs. "Michael, this thing that we do. We do this because we don't care. Why do you suddenly care?"

"I do not care. The job is the same, the consequences are higher now. I need more time."

"Would you like to take me to bed?" she asks shifting the conversation suddenly. "Yes," I reply without hesitation.

"There, see. Between you and I there is an understanding, based on a system, a code. Mutual gratification. Short-term pleasure without long-term problems. We are who we are. It's simple."

"Was this some kind of test?"

"No dear, you can still take me to bed. I'm just trying to show you who you are. When you do your job, you're complete. The size of the job makes no difference."

"You do this because it completes you?"

"Of course, it's a job Michael. A job like any other that defines our place in the universe, our role in creation. Pleasure and pain, life and death. Do well what you enjoy and you will enjoy what you do. Even if it hurts."

She stands up and walks into her bedroom. After a moment, I follow.

Jullian, like usual, is trying to change me. He's drunk, though, and that's how he gets. The bar is called Hole. It used to be called Red's, but that was fifteen years ago. We used to come here when we were younger and we both lived in Boston. I asked him to meet me here, but now I'm regretting it.

"I'm your brother," he's saying. "It's okay, you can talk to me."

"I just wanted to get drunk with you," I say.

"Yeah, but you aren't drunk." He laughs at nothing.

If anything, the bar is seedier than when we were kids. The combat zone might be full of Starbucks now, but there are still parts of South Boston that will make you shiver. Thank God for it.

"Besides, we used to get drunk," Jullian says, slurring. "We do not get drunk now. We are adults."

"You're drunk."

"That is beside the point. What's going on, Michael?"

"Nothing, Jullian. Can't I even have a drink or two with my brother?"

Jullian is quiet for a while. It's late. Someone is shouting at someone else outside. A fire truck roars by and a dirty bartender is concentrating on late night wrestling.

Jullian suddenly looks around, like he's never seen a bar.

"Wait a minute, Michael, isn't this the place we used to come when we were kids?"

"Yeah."

"Huh, it's changed. It used to be nice."

"No, we just used to be young."

"This is where you met that girl, right, what was her name?"

"Laura," I barely whisper.

"Yeah, Laura. She sang here right? That first night, she sang right here with you."

Jullian stumbles off his stool and stares at a vacant corner of the bar. Nothing there now but a broken neon sign for Miller Beer. His hair is uncombed and his eyes a deep shade of red. When drunk, Jullian looks more like me. Alcohol betrays Jullian's happiness.

"Say, bartender, didn't there used to be a piano? Didn't there?" he shouts.

The bartender ignores him, and after a minute Jullian returns to the stool.

"She sang like a fucking bird, remember, Michael? A Goddamn bird. Whatever happened to her anyway?"

"Moved to Manchester."

"Really, hey that's great," Jullian said.

"She's dead, Jullian. She died."

"Oh, jeez, I'm sorry to hear it. Here, hey bartender, get my brother another drink."

The drinks arrive and Jullian makes a toast. I've had plenty but can't seem to get drunk. I came here tonight to tell my brother everything, to start at the beginning. To make him understand. He was to offer me advice, assurances, like family is supposed to do.

But instead he sits there with red, unhappy eyes.

He raises a glass. "To Laura then! Laura who sang like a fucking bird."

I toast Laura and down the drink in one long, bitter gulp.

Laura is angry. I hadn't expected that. I hadn't prepared for it. I should have, but I'm being careless.

"You want me to do what?" she says.

"Sing."

We are sitting on her sofa in her apartment. She had lit some candles earlier which have burned down to liquid stumps. The evening was quiet, focused. I had brought over some greens and we had made pasta for dinner. A night off for both of us. No blood. No bruises.

Like it used to be.

But then I walked into the fire because I had to. Now, even in the flickering lights, I can see Laura's cheeks color a shade of dark red.

She sits there looking at me for a long time. Her hair is loose and wild.

"Is this a joke?"

"No, I just wondered if you could still sing."

She slaps me. I saw it coming, but let it happen. One of her fingernails scratches my face. She knocks a half empty cup of tea off the end table and the cup shatters against a far wall.

She goes from zero to sixty in two seconds.

"You bastard," she screams. "After all this time, after all you promised!"

Then she cries, long sobs, the kind of sounds a child makes. She opens up and it comes out like a flood, half panic, half anger.

I wish I could back up, tell her to forget about it. But I can't. I have to keep going.

"It was something you had, Laura, that was so strong," I say. My words just sound stupid, but maybe it's because I haven't said them in a long time. "It can bring us back, we can just start by playing and find our way out."

"That's over, Michael," she says, but quietly. Tears stream down her cheeks and her shoulders tremble. "It's too late."

"Laura, listen," I move closer to her on the sofa.

I can feel her heat. Her breath is shallow. She looks up at me, a little girl again, and I want desperately to hold her, to touch her hair and kiss her eyelids.

"This isn't who we are, is it?" I reach out to her, my fingers just inches from her cheek. She nearly smiles. I'm so close.

"Go," she says. She lowers her eyes, wipes her face, stiffens her shoulders.

"Laura, I—"

"This is who I am now Michael. Go."

I sit there, my hand still out, desperate.

"God damn it, Michael, get out! Get out!"

I leave Laura's apartment and walk home in the rain. When I get home I call Frost and tell her I'll do the job.

I'm not angry. I'm beyond that now, beyond anything, any hope and any future.

Three weeks later and I'm sitting in the kitchen with Mona eating a chicken sandwich and sipping wine. I glance up at the clock and notice that I'm due at Frost's in one hour. I will be late.

Mona's playing with the ends of her hair. She's chewing gum. She's like a four-year-old, a stupid sister I never had.

"Where did you grow up Mona," I ask.

She seems startled by the question. "Kansas," she says and laughs.

"What was it like?"

"What do you mean?"

"I mean was it out on a farm somewhere or in a city. Did you run through corn fields. Did your father drive a tractor?"

She's quiet for a while, just looking at me. I wonder how long it's been since someone asked her questions like this. I chew and hold her gaze.

"My father was a cop near Topeka. I've never been to a farm."

"You should."

"Should what? Is something wrong Michael?"

"Go to a farm. My father grew up on a farm. I picked corn and apples every year till I was twelve. Then my grandfather died."

"I'm really not much of a farm girl, Michael."

"Where do your parents live now?"

"They died in a car accident. My aunt and uncle raised me. They live in Rapid City."

I get up from the table and walk upstairs to my room. Earlier, I had stripped my equipment space, packing everything into several trunks. All my clothes are stuffed into trash bags. On my one dresser, there is a small jewelry case and I take out a tie pin Jullian gave me years ago. It's shaped like a musical note. I also take out a strip of four pictures of Laura and I, taken in a photo booth in Asbury Park ten years ago. In one of the photos Laura is kissing my hand and looking up into my eyes.

I put the strip back into the case and toss the case into one of the trash bags.

Finally, I slide $3,000 into an envelope and slip the envelope into my back pocket.

Downstairs, Mona is reading the comics. I come up behind her and lift her up out of the seat by her neck and hair. She weighs next to nothing. I toss her roughly over the kitchen table. She crashes against the sink, jarring her head.

"God, Michael, what the fu—"

I slap her with the back of my hand, splitting her mouth with her own metal lip ring, which leaves a bloody streak across the linoleum floor. She is no longer confused. As she scrambles to get to her feet, her eyes are wide in terror.

"Michael, please!"

I take her by the neck and lift her up against a wall. She is crying now and shaking.

"Leave Manchester Mona. Leave forever. Go to Rapid City. I will be leaving the apartment for several days and when I return if I find you here, I will kill you, so help me God. If I find out that you are anywhere but Rapid City, I will kill you. If you tell anyone about me or that I forced you to leave, I will kill you and your aunt and uncle."

I tell her these things calmly, almost in a whisper, not because I am acting but because I really am calm. I feel like

117

I'm floating in warm water, feeling steady and certain. I keep my voice low and look her in the eyes. She is near passing out, and I push her head into the sink and run cold water on her face.

Spit and blood and eyeliner spin down the drain.

"Oh, God, Michael, oh, God, oh God . . ." she's blubbering.

"You don't know me Mona. You don't know anything."

I let her go and she slides down onto the floor. A black bruise will form over her eye and cheek. I reach into my back pocket and toss the envelope into her lap.

"Don't fuck with me Mona and don't disappoint me," I say and leave the apartment.

Ninety minutes later I'm sitting in Frost's apartment, with Frost and Brad sitting on a sofa in front of me. They are looking at me, waiting. When I arrived I told them that I would not say anything and that if they spoke to me before I told them they could, the deal was off.

This isn't an issue for Frost. She is obviously used to unusual requests. She sees the drama and anticipation, it washes over her like a dog in heat. She's burning.

Brad, however, looks like he will burst. His eyes dart around and he keeps rubbing his hands. Every so often, Frost grips his shoulder or pats his knee, and he relaxes.

I float in an ocean of calm. I close my eyes and think of nothing.

Thirty minutes after I arrive, Frost's buzzer rings. I get up and let Laura in.

"Michael?"

"Hello Laura."

"What is this?"

Several days ago, I had instructed Brad to call Laura and set up an appointment. I had made it clear he was not to tell Laura about me or about Frost. He offered her a great deal of money, and Laura, of course, had come.

I didn't know if Brad had it in him to do as I asked. Any deviation from that plan would have brought this meeting to a quick end. Any mention of my name, anything. But there is nothing and now the day is done.

"Sit, and I'll explain everything," I say. I'm surprised at my even voice. I don't recognize it.

Laura is still sore about our argument. She's cautious.

"Is this about the big job you were considering Michael?"

"Yes. Yes and I wanted to make up for what I said by letting you help me."

She smiles and pats my cheek. "You are sweet." She trusts me. I take her hand and she lets me and I lead her into the living room. Her hand is warm and she squeezes her fingers through mine.

I sit Laura down opposite Frost and Brad. They both sit quietly, watching her. Laura does not find this peculiar. She assumes it is part of the scenario that the client has requested.

Laura's hair is up in a tight bun. She is dressed casually, in jeans and a flannel shirt. I stand behind her.

"Laura, I would like you to meet Frost and Brad."

Laura will exchange some pleasantry with them, something kind and warming, a way to develop a rapport with a client. She'll point out something in the room, a painting or perhaps the view. Then, at some point, she will remove her shoes and she'll say, "So, tell me what you want."

But not tonight, never again.

I reach down and grip the bat. There is no need for any further discussion and I do not want Laura to see her death. I raise the bat quickly and swing in a hard arc. At the last moment, Laura begins to turn and I see the flicker of her left eyelash before the blow hits her just above her neck. Her head jerks forward and she sprawls to the ground in front of Brad and Frost.

They leap up, transfixed.

Laura is not dead. I can imagine the confused and pained

119

look on her face. She stretches an arm forward as though to crawl. I'm sad for those terrible seconds, but glad she never turns back to look at me. I raise the bat, and hit her again. She does not move anymore.

Brad and Frost are hanging onto each other, shaking, like if one let go the other would collapse. They both sink to the floor in front of Laura's body. Brad is trembling, not from fear but from excitement. He reaches into his jeans.

"No," I whisper.

Neither hear me. They have forgotten that I am there.

I flip the bat around and strike Brad, knob end first, just above the bridge of his nose. He falls backward, blood gushing from his nostrils. He pulls his hand out of his pants and tries vainly to stop the bleeding. Amid the pain and wreckage of his face, Brad is grinning. Then he is unconscious.

Brad is no longer important to me so I throw away the bat and kneel down next to Laura.

"How does it feel?" Frost says in a hiss from the other side of Laura's body. "Tell me."

A pool of blood, bright pink in the thin light, has begun to collect under Laura's head. I watch the puddle expand. Her face is down, into the rug. Her hair has come loose.

"Damn you!' Frost rages. "Tell me now. Tell me what you feel!"

I reach out and touch a strand of Laura's hair that has come loose from her bun. It burns my fingers.

I sense that Frost is about to slap me, and I manage to catch her arm three inches from my face. She touches my cheek with her outstretched fingers.

"Tell me," she says, more animal than human.

I look into her pale eyes and squeeze her forearm. In a moment, her hand turns white and my fingers begin to leave deep indents in her skin. She understands what I am doing and sits back on her heels. She continues to look me in the eye.

I put enough pressure on her arm to know it must hurt. She whimpers once, but does not try to pull away her arm. I can feel her bones below the skin, can feel them moving, grinding against each other. A slight twist would snap her forearm.

"Tell me, please," she begs, her eyes pooling up.

I let her go and stand up. "Nothing," I say quietly.

She sits there staring at her arm as the color returns to her skin.

"Where are you going? What's going on?." She's not angry yet. She will be, but not yet. For the moment, she's just confused.

I walk into her bathroom and tear down her shower curtain. It's made of thick plastic and has exotic fish designs. I lay the plastic out next to Laura, and gently roll her body onto the curtain. As Laura's collapsed head roles toward me, I notice her eyes are still open. I close them. It takes a little effort, but I have to tug a clump of Laura's sticky hair off the floor. I tuck it into the heavy plastic.

All through this, Frost is sitting on the floor. Sometimes she looks at me. Other times she looks at her arm. She's pretty fucked up.

I push the couch off the rug and push Laura's body onto it. I take one final look at Laura's face, distorted through the plastic curtain, and roll her body into the rug. I tuck the bat in there as well.

"You, you can't just leave," Frost says. She's on her feet now and not as disoriented.

"Laura is my problem now," I tell her. "Be sure to clean the blood and dispose of the clothes and towels."

"Laura? What do I care about that whore? Finish what you started, what you came here to do."

"Get Brad to a hospital, Frost," I tell her. "I think you'll be okay."

"You won't be paid for this Michael!" she screams as I pick

up Laura's body and drape her gently over my shoulder. "You're not finished!"

"I'm finished."

As the door closes behind me, I look over my shoulder once to see Frost, red with humiliation, standing in a pool of Brad's blood.

Three days later, I'm standing by Laura's grave at the edge of the woods behind my father's house when the police come. I can see the state troopers make the turn at the end of the driveway and begin the approach to the house. There must be half a dozen of them.

I watch my father leave the house and walk toward the police cars. He's wearing rubber knee-high boots and shouting something I can't hear.

When I arrived, he came out to greet me in much the same way.

"Why are you here again so soon?" he asked.

"I won't be long, Pop," I said. "I have something I need to do, then I'll be done."

He nodded, and put on a pot of coffee.

Now, as troopers pour out of their cars and fan out around the property, I watch as one pulls my father down and into the back seat of one of the cars. They want to protect him from me. They can all see me clearly.

I've been hearing things in my head these past few days, Laura's voice I guess. Not singing, but more like a background hum. I've been wondering about my own place in the universe and Laura's whisper has helped me think about it, think about what I really am good at, and what I know I'll be remembered for.

There's no fear left and there's no more blood. There's only Laura's murmur.

I steal one last glance at her grave, lift the bat high on my shoulder so all the cops can see it and begin a deliberate walk toward the house.

The Last Jehu

MY FATHER HAS LOST HIS MIND, and I'm barely holding on.

Warren, New Hampshire, is no place to display this madness. The coach rounds a sharp turn in the one-lane pasture road and I can feel the two right wheels lift off the ground. Somehow my father is able to pull back the horses in time and the carriage rights itself with an angry thump. The leather suspension braces groan as he cracks the whip again just to the left of the lead horse's ear.

Where did he learn to do this? We are careening downhill now, on a straightaway that shoots right into the town's one intersection. We're picking up speed. I manage to pull myself up off the dusty, broken coach seat and crane my head halfway out the window.

He's up there in the perch, a mad Phineas Gage. He's laughing hard, tears running down his face, from the chilly October night or perhaps from insanity.

"Dad!" I scream over the rattle and bang as the 125-year-old carriage rockets through potholes and gravel. The tip of that damned rocket in the middle of the town square comes into view. The rocket. He's heading for the rocket!

Something comes loose from the front wheel—a spoke or two, perhaps? I duck my head back into the coach as the splintered pieces cascade past the window and into the night.

The thing is coming apart right under us. This is all my father's doing. We are going to die.

★ ★ ★

It all started this morning when I found the old man sitting in the coach. Again.

He'd been there for three hours, and the folks from the Society milling about outside the barn were pretty annoyed.

"Dad." I was annoyed as well. We'd been through this a million times. "Dad!"

He just sat there, looking straight ahead, hands in his lap. It took me a few minutes to get up into the coach and take a seat opposite him. The last time I was here was when I was a little girl, when there was just a field where the new development now encroaches, when I used to play the role of both cowgirl and Indian squaw in this rickety relic. Now, the thing was all dust and mold and chipped paint.

If I moved even slightly, I could feel the axles creak. I rubbed the bridge of my nose and could smell the rusty iron of the door bar on my fingers.

My father looked old. His eyes had taken on a milky, dazed gaze like he was about to cry.

I took a deep breath. "Dad," I began slowly, speaking like I would to my four-year-old, "what are you doing?"

This deal with the Warren Historical Society had been years in the making. Everyone in town—hell, in the state—had known about this coach for decades. When I was young, Dad would bring the occasional Concord Coach groupie into the old barn for a look around. I'd peer out the mud room window and watch him swing open the long door like a magician pulling back a sheet to reveal something wonderful. I always watched the eyes of whoever was that day's audience, the odd delight and wonder with which they would react to seeing the wooden dinosaur on display in the middle of the barn, like it was the Smithsonian.

I had assumed that some day the coach would fall into dust and be forgotten. And mostly that happened. After Mom died, a padlock appeared on those doors and the matter was put to rest.

Outside, I heard car doors slamming and words like "crazy" and "senile."

I reached out and touched my dad's hand, his knuckles bony and fingers twisted from years of working on state roads. His hands were warm, but he looked straight through me.

"Just—just wait here," I said stupidly, knowing damn well that he was going to sit there like a stone.

I walked back through the barn and past Emma and Charlotte, my dad's two horses. Emma lifted her head as I passed and gave me a low grunt.

"I know, girl, I know." We hadn't figured out what to do with the horses yet.

The barn doors were closed, so I headed into the mud room, a long hall which connected to the house. As I walked through, I noticed that the hall was filled with piles of newspaper and cords of ancient rotting wood. From there, I stepped back outside and came down the long driveway where the Society folks waited. The flatbed the Society had rented to haul away the coach was already gone.

"What the heck is going on, Kate?" Charlie Steward was never a warm man, even less so after losing the deposit on his tow truck. "This is going to cost us!"

I held up my hand. "I don't know, Charlie. I'll pay for the truck. I'm sorry this happened."

The town supervisor and president of the Society had been difficult to deal with over the past few months, hovering around that barn like there was a great white whale in there.

There had been a furious bidding war for the carriage when word got out that the farm was up for sale, but Charlie led the charge. There's a Redstone Rocket in the town square, a prototype of the one that launched the first Americans into space, and the town was desperate to get something else there as well, at least something that made more sense than a ballistic missile in a tiny New England town.

But Charlie was looking for someone to blame. "This is just like him," he said. "Damn, stubborn fool!"

I wavered for a moment between defending my father and admitting that Charlie was right. I was saved from having to make any decision by Martha, our next-door neighbor—Martha who cared for me after my mom died, who brought my father a casserole every Friday for years until her arthritis got so bad that she couldn't open the oven anymore.

"Don't you bad-mouth Joseph," Martha said, moving in on Charlie like a ninety-year-old bird of prey. Charlie backed off immediately. When Martha's mad, there's no escape. "That stubborn fool in there has been through more in his life than twenty of your lives!"

That made no sense, but I didn't get in her way. She stuck a bony finger into Charlie's double-knit suit. "Joseph will hand over that run-down jalopy when, and if, he damn well feels like it and not a moment sooner!"

Charlie shot me an icy look but turned on his heel and stormed down the driveway. Martha and I stood there watching his Cutlass drive away. Finally, we were alone.

"Thanks for saving me, Martha," I said helplessly.

She squeezed my arm, her tiny, bony hand a familiar feeling. "Sometimes, a man can't let go of things, Kate. Let me go talk to him."

"What is he holding on to, Martha?" I asked. "What does he see in that hunk of junk?"

She didn't turn, but from over her shoulder Martha said,

"Your mother, Kate. He sees your mother." And as she walked into the barn I thought I heard her say. "And he sees you."

Later that evening, after Martha had somehow talked my father out of his latest mess, I sat in the kitchen sipping tea, wondering what I was going to do next, when he walked in and said, "You shouldn't have to pay that vulture. Charlie has plenty of money."

"Dad, it's been a long day, " I said. "I'm just not able to process this anymore."

He sighed and poured himself a cup of tea. After a long silence had settled between us, he said. "You shouldn't have left, Kate."

I considered overturning the table and storming out. "Don't start, Dad."

But he just sank his teeth in. "When are you coming home?"

That was the end of it for me. I slammed my hand on the table. "Home? Look around you, Dad. Everything is in boxes; this house is being sold. What home, Dad? I have nothing here, and neither do you!"

I stormed out into the dark, leaving him sitting at the table, glaring at my back. But after a few minutes of shuffling in the cold driveway, I realized I really didn't have anywhere to go. I wasn't willing to go back inside, so I found myself walking to Martha's. The trail between our properties, the trail we had used as kids, was slight, but in the nearly full moon I was able to manage.

The border connecting the properties was a stream and I got a foot-full making my way through there. But soon it seemed as though muscle memory returned me to my childhood and I climbed over Martha's broken stone wall and found myself at the foot of her thick, red door. I knocked hard, and when she didn't answer immediately I got frustrated and started pounding like a child.

I found myself unable to hold back the tears and finally

gave up. I sat down on her stoop and sobbed. When Martha got there she found me, a little girl again.

"Kate, honey, oh my! Come in, please, Kate!"

I just collapsed in her arms and let her lead me into a home that hadn't changed in decades. I leaned hard on her tiny shoulder as she led me into the front room, where I collapsed on a sofa in front of the fire.

"Would you like some hot chocolate, Kate?"

I just nodded and Martha was gone, leaving me to sink even further into memories of my childhood: the countless nights spent curled up in this room, escaping from the agony of my life just across that stone wall. Over and over, I'd come to her. At first, for the candy and hot chocolate. But then, after Mom died and Dad tuned out, I'd come here for her calm. I'd come here because this was the only place I could be me, the only place I could cry, or talk about school, or hate my father for quietly checking himself out of life after the car crash that killed Mom.

"Here you go, hon." Martha handed me a steaming mug, which I held in both hands and raised to my nose. It had been a long time since anyone had put chocolate syrup in my hot chocolate. "Tell me what happened," she said.

And I let it all spill out, all those years away, moving to Los Angeles to be as far from New England as I could, the baby, the divorce, the resentment. I cried again and realized I hadn't cried in a very long time. Maybe not since Mom died.

When I was done, Martha put her arm around my shoulder and I sank into her, wishing, as I had when I was a little girl, that this was my mother. "Did your father ever tell you how he met Violet, your mother?"

I thought about this for a moment, but came back empty. "My God, Martha. He never did."

She just smiled.

"In 1971, your father worked for the state. Back then, DOT

guys used to help out in the little towns when they had public events, like fireworks displays or parades.

"That summer, that ridiculous rocket in town square was installed, and there was a big Warren Old Home Days ceremony and a parade to go along with it. Your dad was sent to Warren to help with the event, directing traffic, setting up the parade route, that sort of thing.

"He was an engineer back then, and he helped install that monstrosity as well, was one of the few men at the state who could.

"Well, I don't have to tell you that Warren was a backwater back then. Guess it still is. But it did have one thing, and her name was Violet. In those days, she had Charlie's job. And her family, your granddaddy, had something too. That Concord Coach that sits in your father's barn."

"What? That coach came from my mother?"

Martha nodded. "And she was a firebrand, your mother. Red hair, just like you, I guess you know that. And stubborn..." Martha trailed off and for a moment it was like she left me and was back there with my mom and dad. The moment passed and she continued. "Well, your father was in town and that missile was the biggest thing to ever happen to Warren. The governor was here, last time any governor paid attention to us, I imagine. There were old cars and fire trucks, and it seems like every organization in the county showed up. The parade started way up on the Mount Moosilauke Highway and came right into town and around the square.

"Your mother was the grand marshal of that parade—a pretty big deal for a small town back then—and care to take a guess what she drove at the front of that line?"

I sighed. "The coach."

Martha smiled. "She was magnificent, Kate. She managed to hunt down an old coach driver uniform, looked like something one of those Beatles would wear on Sgt. Pepper. Course your mom was young then, and that whole 60s thing was popular so nobody knew any difference. But there she was atop that coach, stealing the show. The governor drove *behind* your mother!"

My father never bothered to tell me any of these things. But then again, since Mom died when I was young, I never bothered to ask.

"So," Martha continued, "there's your dad in the town square. His team helped get that rocket here, and then his team helped put it up. After, they had nothing to do except watch the parade, and in rolls your mother, looking like some kind of hippie queen.

"That old coach was a thing of beauty back then. Your mother had painted these elaborate murals along the doors and the coach itself was bright red with yellow spoked wheels. She had a big feather plume that stood straight up from her riding cap."

Martha shook her head and was silent for a moment, lost in the memory.

"The way your mother looked, Kate, the only reason your father won her over is because he was the first one to get to her. I imagine the whole town was her suitor that day. Anyway, the way he tells it, before that coach was ten yards into the square, Joseph had walked straight up to your mother, announced that she was the finest woman in New England and told her he was going to marry her."

I was stunned. "My father? Did that?"

Martha nodded.

"What did she say? Did she say yes?"

Martha laughed. "Oh heavens no! Not right then. But she did tell him that he could ride in her coach. So that's what he did. He got right in and rode the rest of the way into the square. A week later, he moved to Warren, and well, I guess you know the rest."

We sat there in front of the fire a while and the hot chocolate got cold in my hands. "Did they ride the coach often?" I finally asked.

"Are you kidding?" Martha clapped her hands together. "All the time, all over town. Oh, what a grand couple they made." There was another long silence, before Martha said, "And they planned for you in that coach as well."

I'm confused. "Planned? What does that mean, Martha?"

She turned beet red. "Oh come now, Kate, I'm an old lady. Don't make me spell it out for you!"

"Ohhhhh!" and I turned red too, and soon we were laughing together like two little girls.

My head was spinning as I slowly made my way back to my father's house. I felt like he was a new person, a stranger I now understood. I felt like I was looking at an old photo of my parents when they were my age and full of their own impossible dreams.

My mom had always been just a shadow to me, partly because Dad never talked about her. He was never willing to share with me who she really was to him, what they had together.

But now this house, this town and even that dumb, broken coach suddenly made sense in my head. All those years that I spent angry could have been spent understanding him. I was determined to make up for lost time.

I picked my way slowly through the brush back to the house, but hurried my pace when I heard the sound of horses from the front of the barn. It was 2:00 a.m.

I turned the corner and stopped in my tracks. There, by the light of the moon, sat the coach. My father sat up in the driver cab wearing a long black overcoat and riding gloves, a Yankee Jonathan Harker ready to ride off to meet Count Dracula.

"Dad, what in heaven's name are you doing?" But I was too

loud and my voice spooked the horses, who reared back a bit, and like some ghostly apparition the coach began to move. My father turned to look down at me, eyes wide, a crazy grin on his face.

"Kate! I'll be back in a bit!"

Time seemed to stop for a moment as I watched those wheels turn and the coach begin a slow creep down the drive. I looked up at my dad and could see, could actually see, my mom sitting next to him, brass buttons shimmering in the moonlight. I wasn't letting them go this time. Not again.

"Dad! I'm coming!"

And before the horses could really get the coach moving, I leapt up on the step deck, threw open the passenger door and jumped inside.

"Glad to have you, Kate," I heard my dad yell from above. "Hang on!"

My dad wheeled that coach down the final slope toward town square like a madman. And now here we are.

* * *

He's cracking that whip in short controlled bursts, bouncing up there on that seat like the mad cowboy I used to pretend to be when I was little, imagining Indians hot on our trail.

Our road makes a sharp left and runs parallel to the square. Years ago, the town laid in three in-ground spotlights, God knows why. Who would be passing by this place at night to look up at that missile? Now, only one works, and I can see the rocket's silhouette rising up before us, the moon and the light shining white on white.

The coach is tipping now, the broken wheel wobbling at a crazy angle. But my father keeps the coach moving, the two horses huffing deep and low, breathing in short frantic bursts.

Suddenly I am lifted a foot off the seat as dad misses the turn and pops the coach right up onto the green. I come down on the carriage floor on my hands and knees, lose my balance and sprawl halfway across the seat. He's heading straight for the rocket.

"Dad!" I scream. "Dad, stop, please!"

"Kate, get ready to jump!"

"Are you insane?"

"When I say jump, jump! Get ready!"

He's lost his mind. I grab the handle of the coach door and twist just as my dad makes a course correction and I'm flung against the open door. The whole door comes off and suddenly I'm outside in the cold, my hand still gripping the handle, falling.

I instinctively cover my head and as the ground comes up to meet me, as I tumble, I see the rocket, giant against a black sky.

I hit the soft grass and roll twice before coming to a stop, shoulder bruised and ankle twisted but nothing broken.

And there on the grass of my hometown, I turn to watch my father drive his prized possession straight toward the rocket. The horses won't run directly into the rocket, of course, but they swerve at the last moment and the coach's momentum is too much to make the turn with them The coach tips and slams into the base of the rocket. I can't see my father.

The ancient coach explodes upon impact like it's made of balsa wood. The driver's seat plows into the ground at the base of the rocket, the two right wheels digging deeply into the dirt.

Through the dust and shrapnel, I see my father in the grass. He must have jumped at the last second. He looks dazed. Something goes off like a gunshot and I look up to see that two of the rocket's steel braces are buckling. The rocket groans and begins to pull itself out of its concrete base.

"Dad!" My sore ankle slows me down but I manage to get over to him and get my hands under his arms just as the rocket begins its final journey. "Move! That thing is coming down!"

I half drag him over the wooden debris out of the way as

Warren's main attraction comes crashing down behind us. It hits the ground like an earthquake, the sound of tearing metal and popping rivets echoing through the square.

After a dozen yards my dad goes limp and I can't hold him anymore. We go down and stay down.

I put my hands under his head. "Dad, are you hurt?"

After a long couple minutes, he manages to sit up. "I'm OK, Kate."

I sink down next to him, and he puts his arm around me. The two of us sit there looking out over the shattered remains of Warren Town Common, and the town siren goes off and we know that the police and volunteer firemen will be arriving shortly.

I feel numb. "Dad, how did that happen? How could the rocket come down?"

He shrugs. "I put it up, Kate. I'll decide when it comes down."

"But you wrecked it, Daddy," I say, feeling like a little girl again, feeling like I want to cry. "You wrecked the coach."

"Yup," he says and starts to laugh, and soon I'm laughing as well. "Hell of a ride, Kate. That was a hell of a ride!"

My dad pulls me close to him and squeezes my shoulder, and I suddenly feel like I can start again, like I've finally come home.

About the Author

DAN SZCZESNY is a long-time journalist and writer living in New Hampshire.

His first book, *The Adventures of Buffalo and Tough Cookie* (Bondcliff Books, 2013), is a hiking memoir about a one-year, 225-mile journey through some of New Hampshire's least known wilderness areas with his 10-year-old foster daughter. His second book, *The Nepal Chronicles*, about his marriage in Kathmandu and a month-long honeymoon trek to Everest Base Camp, was published in 2014 by Hobblebush Books. *Sing* is his first collection of fiction.

Dan began his career in Buffalo, New York. Since then, he has written for a wide variety of regional and national publications, including the *Main Line Times*, *Philadelphia Weekly*, *Princeton Packet*, *Pennsylvania Magazine*, all4woman.com, *Yahoo! Parenting*, and *Huffington Post*. He writes a weekly column for Good Men Project called "Modern Dad" about getting kids into nature and the challenges of being an older dad.

He's a member of the Appalachian Mountain Club's 4,000-footer club and has written extensively about the outdoors and hiking. He has camped in the Grand Canyon and through-hiked England's Coast to Coast Trail.

He lives in Manchester, New Hampshire with his wife Meenakshi and daughter Uma. For more information about the author, visit www.danszczesny.com.

THE HOBBLEBUSH GRANITE STATE
SHORT STORY SERIES

*Hobblebush Books publishes one or more New Hampshire
short story writers each year, writers whose work has already
received recognition but deserves to be more widely known.
The editors are Sidney Hall Jr. and Kirsty Walker.
For more information, visit the Hobblebush
website: www.hobblebush.com.*